THE PHANTOM VIRUS

Books by Mark Cheverton

The Gameknight999 Series
Invasion of the Overworld
Battle for the Nether
Confronting the Dragon

The Mystery of Herobrine Series: A Gameknight999 Adventure
Trouble in Zombie-town
The Jungle Temple Oracle
Last Stand on the Ocean Shore

Herobrine Reborn Series: A Gameknight999 Adventure
Saving Crafter
The Destruction of the Overworld
Gameknight999 vs. Herobrine

Herobrine's Revenge Series: A Gameknight999 Adventure
The Phantom Virus
Overworld in Flames (Coming Soon!)
System Overload (Coming Soon!)

The Birth of Herobrine: A Gameknight999 Adventure
The Great Zombie Invasion (Coming Soon!)
Attack of the Shadow-Crafters (Coming Soon!)
Herobrine's War (Coming Soon!)

The Gameknight999 Box Set
The Gameknight999 vs. Herobrine Box Set (Coming Soon!)

The Algae Voices of Azule Series
Algae Voices of Azule
Finding Home
Finding the Lost

AN UNOFFICIAL NOVEL

THE PHANTOM VIRUS

HEROBRINE'S REVENGE
BOOK ONE
<<< A GAMEKNIGHT999 ADVENTURE >>>

AN UNOFFICIAL MINECRAFTER'S ADVENTURE

MARK CHEVERTON

SKY PONY PRESS
NEW YORK

Sky Pony Press books may be purchased in bulk at special discounts for sales promotion, corporate gifts, fund-raising, or educational purposes. Special editions can also be created to specifications. For details, contact the Special Sales Department, Sky Pony Press, 307 West 36th Street, 11th Floor, New York, NY 10018 or info@ skyhorsepublishing.com.

Sky Pony® is a registered trademark of Skyhorse Publishing, Inc.®, a Delaware corporation.

Visit our website at www.skyponypress.com.

10 9 8 7 6 5 4 3

Library of Congress Cataloging-in-Publication Data is available on file.

Cover design by Owen Corrigan
Cover artwork by Thomas Frick
Technical consultant: *Gameknight999*

Print ISBN: 978-1-5107-0683-5
Ebook ISBN: 978-1-5107-0680-4

Printed in Canada

ACKNOWLEDGEMENTS

As always, I'd like to thank my family for their support through all my crazy writing binges and Skyping with schools and radio interviews and . . . It seemed endless at times, but their support has helped me to make it through without going too crazy. Credit should go to my editor, Cory Allyn, and the great people at Sky Pony Press. They all help to polish up the story and make it really sparkle. These books would be just a dim reflection of themselves without their help. To all my readers who have taken Gameknight999, Crafter, Digger, Hunter, Stitcher, and Herder into their hearts: thank you for all your support.

A big THANK YOU goes out to Shari Thomas for her dedication and kindness, and to Hilary Northrop for her ever-present smile and magic gum; you two are our heroes. Another big THANK YOU goes to Inge Jacobs for her constant help, support, and understanding. And a gigantic hug and THANK YOU is saved especially for Christine Jones, whose tireless efforts and dedication help countless children. We are forever in your debt.

Our choices and actions define who we are and how others see us. Do people see the real you, or just the convenient you?

CHAPTER 1
SIGNS

The blinding sphere of light slowly faded around Gameknight999, and he could see the blocky landscape that now surrounded him. A long stream of water fell from an outcropping high overhead, forming a small pool of water at his feet. The spray from the water felt cool on his skin. Wiping the moisture from his face, Gameknight felt a flat cheek under his stocky rectangular fingers. He held his hand out in front of him and spread his fingers wide. They were like long, square sausages. He grinned.

That falling water had probably saved his life when he'd first entered Minecraft. He could still remember that first terrifying battle with the giant spider. The monster had carelessly jumped into the flowing water in an attempt to attack him. Trapped in the turbulent liquid, the spider had been unable to defend itself, allowing Gameknight to finish it off . . . his first kill. *What a terrible way to remember your first adventure within Minecraft: the death of another creature,* he thought, his grin fading.

"Are you just gonna stand there looking like an idiot until the sun sets and the monsters all come out to greet you?" a voice said from behind.

Gameknight turned to find his friend, Hunter, standing there in full diamond armor, her red curls spilling out from under the shining helmet. Waves of iridescent magic flowed across the glacial blue coating, casting a soft purple glow around her feet and bathing the nearby oak in sparkling light. Behind her, Gameknight could see two horses tied to a fencepost sticking up out of a clump of grass. The horses were happily leaning down and munching on the thick green blades.

She looked up over his head, and Gameknight knew she was looking at the letters floating in the air above him; this signified him as a user. Craning her head up even higher, Hunter searched for the server thread that would attach to the top of his head and extend up into the sky. The server thread connected any normal user to the server, allowing him to play the game from the physical world. But Gameknight knew he had no server thread. He was not just playing the game; he was actually *in* the game. All of the feelings and smells and sounds that happened within the game were very real to him. With his father's invention, the digitizer, Gameknight999 had been transported into Minecraft and was now part of it. He was the User-that-is-not-a-user.

"Oh . . . ah . . . yeah, I'm ready," Gameknight said clumsily. "It's always a little bit of a shock coming back into the game using my father's invention."

"I thought he smashed it after he captured and destroyed Herobrine," Hunter said.

She untied the horses and handed one of the ropes to Gameknight.

"No, he just demolished the computer that ran the digitizer. It was no problem hooking a new computer up to the digitizer and loading the software."

"You sure the Herobrine virus was completely destroyed?" Hunter asked.

Gameknight nodded.

"He's toast," he said proudly.

"Toast?"

"Oh, yeah, um . . . toast is what you get when you heat up bread," Gameknight explained. "The surfaces of the bread get cooked and turn brown and . . ."

"I stopped listening to your explanation after you said 'toast,'" she said. "You should just make reference to things that are in Minecraft. How would I know what 'toast' is?"

"Good point. But yeah, Herobrine is still destroyed," Gameknight said. "He'll never hurt us again."

She sighed, but in a good way, and Gameknight could see her visibly relax. Reaching into her inventory, she tossed him his armor and weapons. He quickly put them on, then drew his enchanted sword and held it up into the air. Sadly, Gameknight always felt better when he had a sword in his hand.

"Then let's get moving," Hunter said. "Herobrine might be gone, but I still feel better when we're close to the village."

"Me, too," he said as he leapt up into the saddle, Hunter following closely behind. "I know that Herobrine's gone, but I can't help still feeling nervous. We've been living under the threat of total destruction for so long, it's hard to just turn off feeling scared, like it was a switch."

They spun their mounts around and headed out of the shallow basin toward the distant village. Hunter kept her enchanted bow in her hand as they rode. Even though it was daytime and it was unlikely that they'd be attacked, Gameknight knew that she always liked being prepared.

They rode in silence, moving through the blocky landscape at a gentle trot. Soon the lush, rolling hills of the grassland biome gave way to a thick oak forest. It was quiet in the forest, too; the only sound was the clip-clop of the horses' hooves. Gameknight would have expected to hear the occasional moo of a cow or bleat of a sheep, but there was nothing. Was it just nerves making him so suspicious, or was something actually going on?

"You hear that?" Gameknight asked.

"What?" Hunter relied.

"I don't hear any sounds at all," Gameknight said. "Something's wrong. We have to hurry back."

"What are you talking about?" Hunter said. "Herobrine is gone, and I don't see any monsters anywhere. There's a difference between having frazzled nerves and actually doing something silly because of unfounded fears. Do you really think that problems always happen when you come into Minecraft? Aren't we a little self-centered?" She gave him a silly look, crossing her eyes, then laughed. "Relax, there's nothing wrong."

"I'd still feel better if we got to the village sooner rather than later."

Kicking his horse, Gameknight shifted to a gallop as he steered around the thick trunks of the oak trees. Hunter accelerated and matched his speed. As they rode, Gameknight continually looked left and right, ready for a skeleton or spider or zombie to jump out and attack. But nothing happened. Finally, a cow mooed in the distance, and Gameknight999 relaxed a little, glad to hear the animal's voice.

When they reached the end of the forest, the sun was nearing the horizon. Long, dark shadows crept out from the base of the forest trees, stretching across the grassy plain ahead like spooky fingers.

Gameknight smiled and relaxed a bit when he saw the village; after so many adventures inside of Minecraft, it actually felt a bit like home. A high cobblestone wall surrounded the collection of buildings, with tall archer towers standing vigilant along the fortified barricade. Urging their horses across the plain, they headed for the wooden bridge that spanned the village's moat and led to the open twin iron gates.

To the side of the village, Gameknight could see his own castle. Dark purple-black walls of obsidian circled the central keep, forming a perimeter. The cobblestone and obsidian structure that sat at the center of the castle rose high above the barricade. It narrowed as it climbed to the sky, until there was just the smallest of rooms at its peak.

Around the castle, defenses jutted out from the midnight walls, but Gameknight could see that none were manned. Since the destruction of Herobrine, life inside Minecraft had been peaceful, with axes and hoes replacing swords and bows.

"You see, I told you nothing was wrong," Hunter said. "All is as it should be. The great Gameknight999 has no monsters to slay and no great battles to win. All this peace and quiet is making you restless!"

Gameknight harrumphed as he put away his own enchanted bow and crossed the wooden bridge that led across the moat. Dismounting, he held the reins of his horse and walked through the double doors, uncertain what to expect.

Suddenly a rocket streaked up and exploded in a shower of color high overhead. Gameknight jumped in surprise, his hand instinctively reaching for his weapon, but instead of screams, cheers echoed off the walls and buildings as the villagers emerged from behind the wooden homes, shouting his name and smiling. Gameknight frowned slightly at being so jumpy as he dismounted. A young girl came running up, her curly red hair bouncing about her shoulder with every step. She jumped into his arms, a huge smile on her face.

"Gameknight!" she yelled.

"Stitcher . . . I'm glad to see you too," he replied as he caught Hunter's younger sister in his arms.

"She seems happy to see you. We all are," a young NPC said.

Gameknight set the girl down and turned to the villager. The young boy was clothed in a black smock, a gray stripe running down the center. The dark clothing made his blond hair seem to glow with a golden light. The only thing that could possibly be brighter were his shining blue eyes.

"Crafter, my friend, it is so good to see you again," Gameknight said.

The young NPC smiled and nodded. "We are all happy you have returned," Crafter replied. "I thought perhaps a celebration might be in order. Later we'll . . ."

"Gameknight! Gameknight!" A lanky boy was running full-speed toward him.

"Slow down, Herder!" Gameknight shouted, but it was too late.

The young boy tried to skid to a stop, but instead smashed into the User-that-is-not-a-user, knocking him to the ground. Crafter helped the boy up as a pair of large hands reached down and helped Gameknight to his feet. Looking up, the User-that-is-not-a-user found Digger standing over him.

"Is everyone OK?" Digger asked, his booming voice sounding like distant thunder.

"Yeah, I'm OK," Gameknight replied. "Herder, are you all right? What were you thinking, charging toward me like that?"

"Come quick, come quick, there's something wrong with my pigs and cows," the lanky boy said.

Spinning around, Herder streaked to the animal pens, his long black hair flying behind him like a long stringy flag. Gameknight looked at Crafter and smiled, then followed the boy.

They were all shocked when they reached the pen holding the village's pigs. The little pink animals were all walking backward, something that was impossible in Minecraft.

"What's going on here?" Gameknight asked, looking at Crafter.

"I don't know," the young boy replied. "I've never seen pigs do this before."

"Look, there's a sign in the middle of the pen," Digger said. The stocky NPC moved around to the side of the pen so he could see the writing.

"What does it say?" Crafter asked.

Digger looked back at his friends, a confused look on his face.

"I don't understand it," Digger said.

"What does it say?" Hunter asked, having now joined the group.

"Well . . . it says 'KROP'?"

Gameknight laughed.

"What's so funny?" Crafter asked.

"Read it backward," he replied.

Crafter thought about it, then smiled.

"And look at the cows!" Herder yelled, pointing to the brown spotted animals.

Gameknight turned and ran to the cow pen. He didn't need to get that close to see what was wrong. The animals were upside down, moving along on their backs, their long legs waving around as they slid through the pen.

"There's another sign," Hunter said as she streaked by. "It says . . . 'COM'?"

Gameknight laughed again.

"What is it this time?" Crafter asked when he reached his friend's side.

"It's upside-down," Gameknight explained. "Turn it over and it spells . . ."

"COW," Hunter growled. "Well I, for one, don't think any of this is funny."

"Well, your village has been trolled," Gameknight explained. "I don't know how a user did this though, without—"

"Everyone, come back to the gates!" a young voice shouted from the fortified wall.

Gameknight looked toward the voice and saw Stitcher standing at the iron doors, her enchanted bow in her hand, arrow notched and drawn. He ran to his friend and drew his own bow, notched an arrow, then slowly stepped through the doors. He could see a sign sitting on the far side of the wooden bridge. Moving cautiously to the sign, he looked at it and was confused. It was an arrow pointing out onto the grassy plain. He cautiously followed the directions, blades of grass swishing against his diamond boots as he walked. Back from the village, he could still hear the cows and the pigs in the village, the animals apparently not adversely affected by the prank.

Ahead, Gameknight spotted a bare patch of dirt where once there had been grass. As he approached, a sign appeared out of nowhere. Moving closer to the wooden marker to see what it read, Gameknight felt a drop of liquid hit the top of his head. *That's weird*, he thought. *I didn't notice any rainclouds.* He reached his hand up without looking, and when he pulled it back in front of his face, he stopped dead in his track. It was green slime! Stepping back, Gameknight looked all around and saw a heavy rain of green spheres falling, but only in a two-block radius around the sign. *This is impossible*, he thought. *Why are all of these weird things happening?*

He heard footsteps from behind, and knew his friends had caught up to him. Staying outside of the green hail, Gameknight moved so that he could read the sign.

"What does it say?" Crafter asked.

Gameknight glanced over his shoulder. His friends were spreading out across the grassy plain, their weapons drawn.

Looking back at the sign, he read the message. His blood turned to ice.

"Well?" Hunter asked. "You gonna share with us, or keep this a secret?"

He stepped backward, shaking his head.

"It says 'IF YOU THINK I'M DONE WITH U, THEN UR ALL FOOLS!'" Gameknight said.

"Who wrote it?" Crafter asked.

Gameknight turned and looked at his friend. He knew his face betrayed the sense of fear that filled his entire being.

"Are you all right?" Crafter asked.

Gameknight shook his head. "It's signed 'HEROBRINE'!"

CHAPTER 2
SPIDERS

The giant spider watched as the User-that-is-not-a-user struck the sign with a diamond pickaxe, shattering it into a million pieces. The villagers then built a cobblestone structure around the blocks that were covered with the sticky green balls of slime. Sakkir glanced over at the spider next to her, also hidden amid the leaves of the tall oak.

"Saztin, there issss our enemy, Gameknight999," Sakkir said, her eight spider eyes glowing red with hatred.

"Yessss, I can ssssee," Saztin said. "We musssst report to the queen, quickly."

"Agreed," Sakkir replied. "But let ussss wait until the villagerssss have returned back to their village."

The two spiders moved farther back into the leaves and branches, waiting for the NPCs to retreat behind their fortified walls. The villagers quickly finished the cobblestone structure, out-lining the area of the Maker's prank so that the other idiotic two-legs could avoid getting hit by the slime balls. Sakkir noticed that the foolish villagers looked afraid of Herobrine's message, especially the User-that-is-not-a-user. This made the spiders smile. Finally, satisfied that they had walled off the strange green rain, the NPCs returned to their village, the sun slowly setting beyond the horizon. The spiders were free to make the return trip to their queen, Shaivalak.

The two giant monsters moved across the treetops, their long black legs almost a blur as they ran. When they reached the edge of the forest, the duo lowered themselves down on long thin strands of filament until they touched the ground. Around her, Sakkir could hear zombies nearby, their pathetic moaning filling the air.

"You notice how they're alwayssss complaining?" Sakkir said to her companion.

"Yessss, the zombiessss only perceive that which issss bad," Saztin replied. "They cannot appreciate the beauty of the morning dew on a web."

"Or a cloudlesssss ssssky," Sakkir added.

Satzin nodded her large head. She glanced in the direction of the moaning and saw a handful of zombies shuffling through the darkness, their arms always extended out before them.

"Let ussss be going," Saztin suggested.

Sakkir nodded. Her eight eyes glowed with annoyance at the presence of the whining green creatures. They headed northeast toward the hidden cave where their queen waited, traveling through many biomes of grassland, forest, desert, and frozen river. It would take them at least two days to traverse the surface of Minecraft and reach their destination, but they had no choice; they had to report back what they had witnessed. The sisters momentarily considered returning to their own spider nest to feast on the moss that had been collected by the brothers (cave spiders). But their instructions had been to return to Herobrine's cave of devices and report to their queen, Shaivalak, when the User-that-is-not-a-user was found. This was important and there could be no delay, even if it cost them their lives.

After a day and a half of travel, Sakkir had become extremely hungry. She looked at Saztin and could tell that she, too, was starving.

"What if we can't make it?" Sakkir asked in a hoarse, cracking voice.

"You mean, if we sssstarve?" Saztin replied.

The spider nodded, her eyes barely glowing at all.

"Let ussss jusssst try to make it to the top of the next hill," Saztin said, her voice weak.

Sakkir nodded, then charged up the sand dune in front of them. When they reached the crest and looked down upon the landscape ahead of them, they saw the end of the desert and another forest beyond the sand. Both spiders sighed with relief when they saw tall spruces in the forest. The ground was covered by dirt that was a mixture of dark brown and soft orange. Leafy ferns decorated the shadowy corners of the forest, their fronds reaching out to absorb the scant sunlight that made it to the ground.

"There will be food there in the mega taiga biome," Sakkir said as she scurried down the backside of the dune, her sister fast on her eight heels.

The two spiders moved down the hill and across the forest floor until they reached a collection of mossy cobblestone. Quickly, the spiders pulled off the green strands of moss and stuffed them into their mouths. The soft verdant material instantly rejuvenated the monsters' HP, giving them renewed strength. The creatures sat by the stone blocks until they were picked clean, all traces of the green moss eaten.

"Hurry, we musssst get to Shaivalak and report," Saztin said, her voice now strong and clear.

"Agreed," Sakkir replied, feeling rejuvenated.

The two spiders continued their journey through the forest. In the distance, they could hear the howl of wolves, but fortunately, none of them came near. They scurried through the forest until it ended at the multicolored mesa biome.

"We're getting closssse," Sakkir said. "I can feel her."

"Yessss," hissed Saztin.

They ran across the brown, orange, and tan sands like two fuzzy shadows. They knew their dark bodies would be easy to spot against the colorful sand and clay, but they had no choice. Moving as fast as they could, the pair of monsters sprinted across the mesa. In the distance, they could see grassland and an extreme hills biome butting up against the green rolling hills; that was their target. The secret cave would be there, hidden under the massive mountain that loomed on the horizon.

When they reached the end of the mesa, the spiders moved onto the grasslands, heading toward the distant hills. But as they reached the tall grass, they could feel a rumbling in the ground.

"Horsssssessss," Sakkir said to her companion.

"They'll catch ussss," Saztin said.

"You musssst divert them sssso that I can make it back to the queen," Sakkir commanded.

The spider sighed, then turned and changed directions, away from her sister. Saztin knew, as the younger of the two, this task must fall to her.

"Good-bye, Saztin," Sakkir said in a sad voice. "You sssserve the queen and the nesssst with strength and obedience."

Her sister nodded her large black head, then turned and ran toward the thundering hooves.

There was a sense of pride in Sakkir's voice as she watched Saztin move off through the tall grass to play a deadly game of hide-and-seek with the approaching mounted warriors. Sakkir knew her sister would not survive, but would make the villagers chase her in the opposite direction so that she could report to their queen.

As she ran, the spider could feel the vibrations from the horses slowly fade as her sister drew the villagers away. Her sacrifice would allow the news to make it to their spider nest.

Once she reached the extreme hills biome, Sakkir scurried toward the gigantic mountain that dominated the landscape. She followed her intuition, or the spider queen's commands—it was hard to tell which sometimes—to the secret tunnels. As the spider followed the twisting passages, she could feel the presence of the queen getting stronger in her mind. Sakkir moved faster and faster until she finally reached a large cavern lit with redstone torches on the walls. At the far end of the cave, the orange light of lava lit the cave walls, showing how truly immense this chamber really was: at least thirty blocks wide at the center and a hundred from end to end.

Sakkir moved through the entrance and stepped onto a narrow bridge of stone only a single block wide. It led to a large, round platform of cobblestone. Glancing over the edge, the spider could only see darkness below, the depth of the chamber so great that the bottom was not even visible. Scurrying across the platform, Sakkir found the queen perched near the wall of the cave, her small form appearing to float in midair as she dangled from a fine strand of web.

"What do you report?" the spider queen asked, glaring down with purple eyes.

"Shaivalak," Sakkir said, bowing her head low to the ground. "I have sssseen your enemy."

"What issss thissss?" the ruler asked.

"The Usssser-that-issss-not-a-ussssser hassss been ssssspotted," Sakkir said.

Reaching up, Shaivalak severed the web from which she was hanging with one of her curved claws. She landed gracefully on the ground and approached her subject.

"You ssssaw him?" she asked.

"Yessss, Shaivalak," Sakkir replied.

A skeleton stepped out of the shadows and approached the two spiders. He wore a crown of bones on his head and had an evil look in his cold, dead, eye sockets.

"It is time," Reaper, the skeleton king, said.

"Indeed," replied Shaivalak.

"The message from Herobrine, before he went to the physical world, said we were to activate the device when the User-that-is-not-a-user appeared again," Reaper said, as if he were reciting from a book.

"I know what hissss final commandsssss were," Shaivalak said, contempt in her voice.

Standing, the spider queen scurried across the cobblestone platform, moving toward the dark side of the chamber. Reaper followed close behind, curious as to what Shaivalak was doing. She moved across the narrow bridge that connected the cobblestone platform to a shadowy stone plane that had strange orange blocks distributed across it. Weaving her way around the blocks, the spider queen moved to a lever that had been placed on the wall, a hole in the sheer rock nearby. She reached up and placed one of her wicked, curved claws on the mechanism, then looked up at the skeleton king, her eyes glowing bright purple.

"Thissss issss the lasssst great revenge of Herobrine," Shaivalak said as she pushed the lever.

Instantly, redstone lamps flared to life, revealing a counter glowing high overhead. The display was massive, at least a dozen blocks tall and easily visible from anywhere in the cave. The blocks moved on hidden pistons, forming the number 100. Another piston allowed molten stone to spill out of the hole in the wall of the cave. The lava fell into a pool lined with stone, the container nearly empty, but now filling with the deadly liquid. Above the hole was a redstone lantern that pulsed a slow tempo, as if it were a beating heart.

"When the pool fills with lava," Reaper said, "Herobrine with have his revenge, and the villagers and Gameknight999 will feel his wrath one final time before they are all destroyed."

He turned away from the display and looked down at the fuzzy spiders.

"Shaivalak, what do you think the Maker is doing to the pathetic users in the physical world?" the skeleton king asked.

"He issss making them ssssuffer. I have no doubt."

"I would love to see it," Reaper said. "It must be glorious. I'm sure the User-that-is-not-a-user is here in Minecraft to try and hide from the destruction of his home world."

"The sssskeleton king issss likely correct," Shaivalak replied.

"Are you sure your spiders are out there looking for him?" the skeleton king asked.

"My warriorssss will sssstop him from ever reaching thissss cave," Shaivalak said proudly. "But you musssst bring your sssskeletonssss and guard thissss chamber."

Reaper looked down at the spider and nodded.

"I will go and bring my finest warriors. If he manages to get past your spiders, then my skeletons will stop him here. And I hope your sisters do fail, for I look forward to destroying the great Gameknight999 myself."

The skeleton king laughed a dry, rattling laugh as he headed for the chamber exit, Shaivalak clicking her mandibles together with evil delight.

CHAPTER 3

DESERT SNOW

Gameknight999 did experiments on the backward-walking pigs and upside-down cows to find out if the animals themselves had been altered permanently. He attached a leash to one of the cows and led the creature away from the COM sign. When it was a few blocks away, the animal quickly climbed to its feet, unharmed. In fact, it appeared as if the cow were unaware that anything was amiss. But when it was led back into the pen, the spotted bovine instantly flipped over and moved on its back again.

"There's nothing wrong with the cows," Gameknight announced to Crafter. "It's the location that's making them act weird."

"Just like with the pigs," the young NPC said, nodding his head. "But how can Herobrine be doing this? You said he was destroyed."

"He was. I saw my dad destroy the computer he was trapped in. There was no way for that virus to escape into the Internet." Gameknight closed the gate to the pen and stepped away from the cows. He remembered what Hunter had told him outside the village, that believing things that couldn't be true just because he was scared was silly. What was happening with the pigs and cows and green rain was really strange, but it didn't mean that Herobrine was responsible. He couldn't be. "And even if he had somehow escaped into the Internet, he would have already done terrible damage to things to the physical world and we'd have heard about it." Gameknight turned away from the cows and brought his gaze down to his friend's bright blue eyes. "I'm telling you, Herobrine is dead."

"Then how can he be causing these pranks?" Crafter asked.

The User-that-is-not-a-user shook his head.

"I don't know," Gameknight said. "But if . . ."

Before he could finish his thought, NPCs came running out of the cobblestone watchtower that loomed high over the village.

"Someone's come," one of the villagers said to Crafter. "They need our help."

"What is it?" Gameknight asked.

"Just come and hear his story," another villager said.

Crafter and Gameknight looked at each other, confused, then ran to the watchtower. When they reached the tall cobblestone structure, they dashed inside, heading to the far corner of the floor. A block had been removed, revealing a long vertical tunnel that sank deep into Minecraft. Crafter stepped into the hole and slid down the ladder that was attached to one wall, disappearing into the darkness. Gameknight moved to the passage and followed his friend down the shaft.

At the bottom of the ladder was a straight horizontal tunnel. Torches dotted the walls of the passage, each casting a circle of illumination that pushed back the darkness. Gameknight followed Crafter, who was four strides ahead of him. They passed through the tunnel in silence, uncertainty slowly filling Gameknight's mind.

What is it now? Did some piece of Herobrine survive? Or was it the monster kings that Herobrine created? Questions circled through Gameknight's mind like hungry vultures.

They reached the end of the tunnel and came to a large circular room with a pair of iron doors on the far side. This was the room where Gameknight had first met his friend Crafter. It seemed like a million years ago.

"Come on," Crafter said from the iron doors.

Gameknight realized he had stopped in the center of the room and was lost in thought, reliving the memory of that first meeting.

"Sorry," he replied and stepped to the door.

Crafter drew his sword and banged on the door with the hilt. Instantly, a group of armored warriors appeared on the other side, their shining iron armor showing through the small barred window set in the center of each door. Upon recognizing the visitors, the entryway was opened and the warriors stepped aside. Gameknight and Crafter stepped down the stairs and onto the crafting chamber floor. As they descended, Gameknight looked at the activity around him. For the first time in a long time, the workers in the chamber were crafting something other than weapons and armor. There were saddles being made, and boats, and fences . . . all the things that Minecraft needed when all was peaceful.

Near the foot of the stairs, they found an NPC leaning against a block of stone. He wore a gray smock with a white stripe running down the center. Gameknight noticed many tiny scars on his fore-arms, as if he'd been cut by a hundred tiny knives.

"Stonecutter," Crafter whispered as they approached.

Gameknight nodded his understanding; that was this villager's job, and his name as well.

"Stonecutter, what brings you to our village?" Crafter asked.

The visitor stood to face Crafter, but his eyes were focused on Gameknight. The NPC looked up at the letters floating over his head, then even higher to look for the server thread that was not there. A look of wonder came over the villager as he realized who was standing before him.

"Stonecutter, what is wrong?" Gameknight asked. "Why are you here?"

"Ohh . . . ummm . . . oh yeah, I was sent here by my crafter," Stonecutter said. "Something strange is happening to our village and we need help."

"What's wrong?" Crafter asked.

"Actually, I don't know," the villager replied. "I was in our crafting chamber, and the crafter and village leaders came down and sent me to your village to find help. My crafter told me very little, mainly, that we needed you," he said, gesturing to Crafter, "and the User-that-is-not-a-user to come and help us."

"What's all this about?" a voice said from behind.

Gameknight didn't need to turn around. He would recognize the voice of Stitcher, Hunter's younger sister, anywhere.

"Yeah, what's going on?" Hunter added.

The sisters walked up to Crafter and Gameknight. By now, the legend of the redheaded sister archers had spread across Minecraft, and by the look of shock on the stonecutter's face, he clearly recognized them.

"What did your crafter tell you?" Gameknight asked.

"All he said were three words: 'snowballs and bones,'" the NPC replied.

"'Snowballs and bones'?" Gameknight repeated.

The stonecutter nodded.

"We should see if we can help," boomed Digger as he came down the stairs, his big pickaxe in his hands. "But if there are bones, then Herder should come as well. *Bones* can mean only one of two possibilities: skeletons or wolves."

"Digger is right," Crafter said. "We might need Herder. But what about the snow?"

The big NPC shrugged.

Crafter turned and faced one of the workers in the chamber. "Go find Herder and bring him here, please," the young NPC asked.

The worker nodded and took off running. In minutes, Herder had joined the companions.

"Stonecutter, show us to your village," Crafter said.

"OK," the NPC replied.

Placing his minecart on the tracks before him, he shot off down the iron rails into a tunnel that pierced the wall of the crafting chamber. Crafter pulled minecarts from a nearby chest and handed them out, then took off behind the stonecutter, Gameknight close behind.

They moved through the minecart network until they reached the next village, then switched to a new track and headed to the north. In five minutes, they reached Stonecutter's village. When they emerged from the tunnel, Gameknight could instantly feel the tension and fear among the NPCs of this village. It looked as if all of the villagers were inside the crafting chamber, which almost never happened. By the looks on their faces, they were afraid to go back up to the surface.

What had made them so scared? Gameknight thought, and then the word "bones" popped into his mind.

"Are you being attacked by skeletons?" the User-that-is-not-a-user asked the crowd. The villagers shook their heads, fear and panic filling their square eyes.

Gameknight looked at Crafter, confused.

"I think we need to go up and see what's happening," Crafter suggested.

"I think you're right," Gameknight replied.

Once all of his friends arrived, Gameknight led them up the steps and out of the crafting chamber. Moving quickly through the tunnels, they made their way to the watchtower that stood guard over the village. But as soon as they entered, their ears were assaulted by what sounded like a terrible storm raging outside.

Gameknight moved to the window and peered out. He could tell by the gray-green grass that they were in the savannah; bent and twisted acacia trees were visible on the hills that surrounded the community. The landscape on those hills looked peaceful enough, with no monsters in sight, but within the village, it was a different matter. Everywhere inside the fortified wall of the village, it was snowing . . . which was impossible. It never snowed in the savannah. This was the desert. But nevertheless, Gameknight could see the ground was blanketed in snow. Except, as he looked closer, he saw something wasn't quite right. The 'snow' he saw wasn't floating down like fluffy snowflakes; it was plummeting to the ground at high speed.

"Is it hail?" Stitcher asked as she peered through the window.

"I don't think so. Look at the shape," Hunter replied. "Some of them look like snowballs, but others look sorta like sticks."

"They look like icicles falling from the sky," Digger said as he looked through the barred opening in the door.

Reaching into his inventory, Digger pulled out his big pickaxe as well as a second pick. With a tool in each hand, the big NPC looked ready for battle. The image of him with his two picks reminded Gameknight of something he'd seen on the Internet; something about an update to Minecraft.

"We have to go outside and see what it is," Crafter said.

"Hold on a minute. I need to do an experiment," Gameknight said.

"This isn't the right time to be messing around," Hunter said suspiciously.

Gameknight looked at her and smiled, then pulled out a crafting bench and placed it on the ground. Pulling out three blocks of red wool, three planks, and an ingot of iron, he quickly placed them in the arrangement he'd seen on someone's snapshot video. The pieces instantly transformed into one large rectangular object.

"What is that?" Stitcher asked.

Gameknight picked it up and held it in his left hand.

"It's a shield," he explained. "A new update to the game. It must have been finally added. I can use it to go out there and protect myself from all the hail and icicles."

"Good idea," Crafter replied as he pulled out a piece of armor from his own inventory.

Gameknight opened the door and stepped out into the deluge, the shield held over his head. As he moved through the village, it felt as if someone were hammering with a thousand tiny hammers on the metal that sheltered him. Each delivered a small thump, but together, the ferocity of blows made it difficult to keep the shield held high.

"Gameknight, look," Crafter said off to his right.

The User-that-is-not-a-user turned to his friend. Crafter was crouched down, holding an iron chest-plate over his head with one hand and pointing to the ground with the other. Gameknight999 knelt beside him. He was shocked when he realized what was falling from the sky . . . bones! Thousands of bones, mixed with snowballs, were falling all across this village.

"How can this be?" Gameknight asked Crafter.

But before the young NPC could respond, Hunter's voice sliced through the storm.

"SIGN!"

She was standing near the crops, next to a post planted in the ground, right in the middle of what used to be a field of wheat. As he reached her side, Gameknight saw that all the crops were destroyed. The falling bones had crushed the life out of the plants, and the snowballs had frozen the savannah soil solid. Moving behind Hunter, he looked down at the sign.

"What does it say?" boomed Digger.

Gameknight sighed as he read the message out loud.

"The sign says, 'THIS IS YOUR FUTURE.' It's signed by Herobrine again," Gameknight said.

Digger pulled out his pickaxe and shattered the sign in frustration, then immediately began building a cobblestone structure over the fields so the wheat and melons could be replanted.

"How could Herobrine be doing this?" Stitcher asked as she moved near. "We destroyed him. I'm sure of it."

Gameknight shook almost imperceptibly as he thought about Herobrine still being alive. *But that's impossible*, he thought. *It's just some prank.*

"At least this is relatively harmless," Gameknight said, unable to come up with an explanation.

"Harmless? Hardly," Herder said, a look of anger in his eyes. "Look at the crops! They're destroyed. No one will ever be able to live here again."

"Sure, but at least no one was hurt," Gameknight said. "The villagers can build new homes and form a new community. They'll be all right."

"But will Minecraft be all right?" Herder asked, a stern look on his square face. "Minecraft must always be in balance. If we mine too much iron or coal or gold, we throw the natural mechanisms of the land out of balance. Every villager would know not to do that; it would be irresponsible and foolish. After all, why would someone knowingly use up all the resources of a land, leaving it bare? This is the same thing. Minecraft must be kept in balance, and all these bones and snowballs tip that balance in a dangerous direction."

"I don't think these bones and snowballs are going to hurt anything. They're a bit of an inconvenience, but that's all," Gameknight replied.

"You don't understand," Herder replied, his voice edged with anger. "Things like this never seem like a big deal at first because when they first start, they're small. People accept them because they're not very significant. It seems like small steps, but if you take enough small steps, you can go great distances. This feels like the first of many small steps, and if we don't try to figure out what's happening here, soon it may be far too late to stop it."

"Wisdom from the Wolfman," Crafter said, patting the boy on the back.

The lanky boy smiled then looked at his friend, Gameknight999. But the User-that-is-not-a-user was not smiling. He was looking at the rainstorm of bones bouncing off a hastily-built roof of cobblestone to protect the crops, scowling.

"What *is* going on here?" he said to himself, knowing deep down that his friend, Herder, could be right. "This feels wrong, very wrong. Sure, everything so far has been a harmless prank . . . but how long will they stay harmless? And what's going to happen next?"

CHAPTER 4
SENDING A MESSAGE

The spider queen hung high up on the wall of the massive cavern, peering down on all the shadowy blocks spread out across the platform below. There were hundreds of the strange orange-checkered cubes, all of them connected to some kind of red powder. As a spider, Shaivalak had no idea what all of it did, but knew it was somehow an important part of Herobrine's plan for revenge against Gameknight999 and the NPCs of the Overworld.

Herobrine had escaped from Minecraft with the User-that-is-not-a-user; she'd seen it in the Nether during the Last Battle. She assumed the Maker was causing great suffering in the physical world, so why did he need revenge here in Minecraft? It didn't make much sense to her, but she knew it didn't matter. Her job was the follow the Maker's last commands before he escaped, and she would do that to the best of her abilities.

Releasing her grip on the block of web, she slowly crawled down the wall to the cobblestone platform that sat in the middle of the giant cave. At the edges of the platform was a bridge that led onto the cobblestone plane, and a second bridge that led to the platform filled with the strange orange blocks. On either side of the narrow, block-wide bridge, there was nothing but a long, long drop to the bottom.

Gripping the cave wall with the sharp points of her curved claws, the spider queen climbed down below the cobblestone plane that had been built here by the Maker. At the bottom of the cavern, she could see a single redstone torch illuminating a small section of the wall; this was her destination.

Echoes of her claws scraping across the cold stone walls reverberated throughout the silent chamber as she descended. All of the skeletons had been sent away to patrol the upper passages of the cave, leaving Shaivalak alone. That was fine; right now, she only wanted to look at Herobrine's last instructions again. Continuing her descent, she moved down the wall of the cavern as easily as a person would walk on the ground. But it was at least forty blocks from the bridge down to the bottom of the cavern; a fall from that height would be fatal.

When Shaivalak reached the bottom, she scurried toward the redstone torch. Around it sat a series of signs, all of which had been placed there by Herobrine. How or when he'd built this place, she didn't know—maybe during the assault on the Source, or perhaps after her predecessor, Shaikulud, had been destroyed by that cowardly Gameknight999.

She approached the signs and read them all again. They outlined how to defend the cavern by sending the spiders out into the Overworld to watch for the User-that-is-not-a-user, while the skeleton king and his minions would guard the cavern's tunnels and passages. But the most important sign was the one directly under the redstone torch. It told how to start the timer on the device that sat in shadows high overhead: a command block system.

Shaivalak had done that, and could see the timer display on the wall of the cavern slowly ticking down. It currently read 92 . . . a long way from zero.

The sign next to it had only three words, but the spider instantly knew its meaning. It read in big, bold letters: "MAKE HIM SUFFER!"

Her eyes glowing with evil intent, Shaivalak climbed back up the wall to the cobblestone platform. Crawling around the edge, she moved to a cluster of spiderweb blocks and sat on the soft filaments. Reaching out with her mind, she felt for the strange, ethereal threads that connected her to all her spiders, sisters and brothers alike. She wanted to send the brothers, who were all cave spiders, out after Gameknight999 and his companions. Those foolish NPCs never thought to have milk with them, the only antidote to a cave spider's poison, but the brothers were all busy caring for the next batch of spider eggs in the hatchery. No, this would have to be a job for the sisters. Reaching out to her spider minions, she sent instructions of her own that would bring them all to action.

Find the Ussssser-that-issss-not-a-usssser, Shaivalak commanded. *The Maker commandssss that he must be made to ssssuffer. Sssseek him out and punissssh him for his crimessss againsssst the ssssspider nation. Do not return without hissss diamond blade.*

She knew the small groups of spiders would search the Overworld until he was found. They would throw themselves at him and try to destroy him, even though they might find themselves outnumbered. But the instructions were not to destroy him; the Maker's message was clear. The loss of fifty spiders was not important; more would be hatched soon, and those younglings would soon be ready for battle and could replace those that were killed.

All that mattered was that Gameknight999 suffered, and Shaivalak knew her spiders were up for that task.

CHAPTER 5

THE SISTERS ATTACK

Gameknight999 placed the cobblestone blocks across the makeshift roof as quickly as he could; he knew Hunter's arm was likely getting tired. She was holding an iron chestplate over his head while he put the stone blocks down, creating new cover that would span the width of the village. The white bones and snowballs bounced off the iron shield and landed a block away. The force of their impact stung if you didn't hold something over your head, but didn't really do any damage; it was only a nuisance. The only real victims were the village's crops, and they'd been the first to get a new protective cover.

The bone storm had not let up once since their arrival to the savannah village. They still didn't know how Herobrine had managed to cause this to happen, and his tricks were slowly turning from just peculiar to unsettling.

This was his fourth prank, after the pigs, the cows, and the slime balls. Crafter pointed out that the pranks were increasing in severity, which meant that there could be more coming that might actually be dangerous, or even deadly. But how could they help to build up their defenses against a prank that they didn't know the slightest thing about? They'd decided there wasn't anything that could be done immediately that would make them much safer. As a result, it was agreed the first priority was to help this village so that its NPCs could survive.

It had been Herder's idea to put a roof over the entire village. The job was something doable, a confidence booster for the group, plus all the villagers could contribute something by either placing the individual stones or holding an iron umbrella as armor over the builders while they worked. Focusing on what they *could* do rather than what they *couldn't* instantly buoyed the villagers' spirits. The NPCs eagerly gathered stacks of cobblestone and went to work. Operating in pairs, they quickly covered the area around the watchtower, creating stone coverings twelve blocks off the ground that were slowly spreading outward and protecting more of the village with every passing minute.

As the stone roof grew larger, they could fit more pairs of workers on the perimeter, and the roof grew at a faster rate. By noontime, it spanned half the village.

"Come on, faster," Hunter complained. "My arm is getting tired."

"You want to switch?" Gameknight offered. "I'd happily let you lean over all day and lift blocks of stone."

"As attractive as you make that sound, I'm thinkin' no," Hunter replied with a smile. "What we need to do is—"

A voice cut through the clattering noise.

Gameknight glanced up at the watchtower. Stitcher stood up under the new cobblestone roof, staring out into the desert. It looked as if she were pointing at something, but it was difficult to see through the downpour of white debris.

"We better find out what's going on," Hunter said. she dropped the iron shield she'd been holding over Gameknight's head and ran for the watchtower.

Gameknight's diamond helmet started to ring as the bones bounced off the blue crystalline coating and fell around his feet. The snowballs froze his cheeks. Not wanting to stand around waiting to hear what happened, he followed Hunter, careful not to trip or slip on any of the snowballs piling up on the newly-constructed roof. There was a recently-cut doorway into the side of the watchtower, and Gameknight ducked inside, feeling better out of the relentless weather.

Removing his helmet, Gameknight ran up the steps to the top level of the watchtower. There, he found Hunter and Stitcher both peering out into the white storm at the landscape before them. Gameknight stood next to the younger sister.

"What did you see?" he asked.

"I thought I saw something moving across the savannah," Stitcher said. "I don't think it was horses or cows or anything like that; the shape was . . . wrong."

"Then what was it?" Hunter asked.

"I don't know for sure," Stitcher replied. She sounded frustrated. "It was there for a second, then it was gone. Now I can't see anything through these bones."

Gameknight put a hand on her shoulder. She looked up at him and gave him a worried smile, her brown eyes filled with apprehension.

"Stitcher, what do you *think* it was?" Gameknight asked.

"Well . . . they looked like shadows, but they were round, sorta," she said.

"Spiders," Hunter growled.

"Maybe," Gameknight said. "Where did you see them?"

"Over by the river that cuts through the desert," Stitcher said. "That river is in a shallow valley that's maybe four or five blocks deep. The spiders could be running along the banks of that river and we wouldn't be able to see them until they were right on us."

"What do you think we should do?" Hunter asked.

"Well, I think we need to know what's out there," Gameknight mused. "But there's no way we can use the horses in this storm without them panicking. We'll have to go on foot."

"Right," Hunter agreed. "Then let's get going. We can't afford to let the—"

"SPIDERS!" someone shouted through the clattering storm.

Gameknight spun around and saw a large group of spiders scaling the walls of the village behind them. The monsters hesitated for just a moment as they first entered the bone-and-snow storm, as if they didn't really want to, but were being forced to attack.

"Everyone, get off the roof and meet down on the ground!" Gameknight shouted. "Stitcher, seal up the stairways that lead to the ground after everyone is safely down. Let's not make it easy for them to get to us. Use your bows to keep the monsters back."

Not waiting to hear a response, he sprinted down the cobblestone stairs that led to the ground. Terrified villagers greeted him, all of them looking like they wanted to just run away out into the desert.

"No, you can't run. This is your home!" Gameknight cried before anyone spoke. "I know you're scared, but we have to work together, and quickly. Now, everyone pull out some cobblestone. We have about two minutes to build some defenses before the monsters figure out where we are. Build a wall around the watchtower, quickly."

Digger suddenly appeared out of nowhere, his big pickaxe on his shoulder. Without being told, he took charge of the defenses, telling the villagers where to put walls and holes for archers. In minutes, stone walls were sprouting up out of the sandy ground, forming a protective ring around the center of the village.

"No, no . . . we can't just wall ourselves in," Gameknight said when he saw what the villagers were doing. "We have to lure the spiders into a trap so that we can destroy them."

"What do you suggest?" Digger asked.

Gameknight thought for a moment, then remembered the first spider he'd ever battled when he first came into Minecraft.

"Dig a hole here," he said, "then build a wall here with holes along the edge, and then . . ."

Quickly Gameknight explained his plan. The villagers nodded their blocky heads as he spoke, understanding not only what the User-that-is-not-a-user's plan was, but understanding the danger they were all in as well. There was uncertainty in their eyes, but Gameknight knew . . . no, he *hoped* that they would do what they needed to when the time came. All he wanted now was for the spiders to come to them.

"Everyone ready?" he asked.

Blocky heads nodded slowly.

"OK, here we go," Gameknight said.

Moving through the narrow passage they'd just built, he opened the wooden doors that had been placed in the makeshift stone wall. Stepping out, he removed a piece of iron armor. With the flat of his sword, he banged on the iron sheet, creating a loud gonging sound that echoed throughout the village.

"If you want me, you have to come and get me!" he screamed. "The User-that-is-not-a-user is waiting for any spider that might be brave enough to challenge me."

A large, black, fuzzy body climbed around the edge of the cobblestone roof, then moved along the surface, hanging upside down. The monster reached a wall and gracefully crept down it like gravity had no effect on the creature.

"Is that all?" Gameknight asked. "A single spider? Well, it's more than I expecte—"

He hadn't even finished talking before twenty more spiders emerged behind the first, moving like a deadly black wave. They flowed over the edge of the roof, some dropping to the ground while others climbed down the walls.

Putting away his sword, Gameknight drew his enchanted bow and fired it at the monsters. A purple fire appeared on the end of the arrow as it leapt off the bowstring, the *Flame* enchantment doing its magic. As the arrow streaked through the air, two more flew over Gameknight's shoulders to join it. The three blazing arrows all found the same target, and the monster disappeared with a pop as the magical flames consumed its HP.

Gameknight glanced over his shoulder. Hunter and Stitcher stood near the defensive wall, new arrows already notched and ready to fire. The monsters' clicking grew louder as the spiders advanced, their eyes glowing bright red with hatred as they glared at the pile of silk lying on the ground where their comrade had stood only a moment earlier.

One of the dark creatures scurried forward a few blocks.

"Get back behind the wall and be ready," Gameknight called over his back to his friends and the villagers behind him. Then he tightened his grip on the bow in his hand and focused his attention on the enemy in front of him. "Come on, you filthy spiders, come get me . . . if you dare."

Drawing another arrow back, he fired at the lead spider, hitting the monster in the shoulder. The spider shrieked in pain, then charged forward, the rest of the horde following close behind.

Spinning around, Gameknight dashed through the wooden doors, leaving them open as he shot through the long, narrow corridor of cobblestone. He raced past NPCs tucked into every hole and crevice in the walls, their bows drawn back and ready to fire.

"They're coming!" Gameknight yelled as he reached the end of the passage, in clear view of any monster that followed.

Drawing his two swords, he waited. Many of the villagers saw the blades he carried and whispered to each other, their gazes changing from fear to confidence at the sight of the dual weapons.

"Here they come!" someone shouted.

The first spider stepped into the narrow corridor. She saw Gameknight standing at the end of the passage, looking like a fool ready to be devoured, and charged ahead, followed by more monsters. The User-that-is-not-a-user didn't budge. He just stood there, apparently oblivious to the danger in front of him, and this enraged the spiders even more. The creatures surged down the corridor, moving so quickly they didn't notice any of the archer holes carved into the walls, or the two pistons at the end of the passage.

The first spider made it the end of the corridor and reached out for Gameknight, but just as her deadly claws were about to slice him, one of the pistons was activated. The spider toppled over sideways as the piston smashed into her, sending her sliding into a deep hole filled with water.

"Come on, I'm waiting!" Gameknight taunted.

Just then, the second spider reached the other piston and was thrown aside just like the first monster, falling into a pool of water. Archers all around the pool fired down onto the creature, rending its HP in seconds. More spiders charged, all meeting the same fate because they were charging so quickly that they didn't realize the trap that Gameknight had set. Eventually, enough spiders fell into the holes filled with water that those in the rear hesitated to move any closer down the corridor. That was when the archers started to fire through the holes in the walls. Arrows struck them from both sides as the monsters panicked, climbing over each other in a frenzy as they raced to retreat back out of the narrow passage.

"They're escaping!" Digger yelled.

"No, they're not," Gameknight said. "ATTACK!"

The User-that-is-not-a-user charged forward. He moved through the corridor and met the spiders under the cobblestone overhang. The creatures turned on him instantly, but none of them had ever fought Gameknight999 and his two swords. He quickly turned into a spinning weapon of destruction, slashing at the spider to his left, then attacking the one to his right before leaping high into the air, bringing his swords down on the doomed creature directly in front of him. As the spider disappeared with a pop, more villagers flowed out of the passage and fell on the monsters, driving them backward. Flaming arrows whizzed down the corridor between the attacking villagers at the front of the offensive, striking the retreating spiders.

Gameknight and the NPCs had destroyed many spiders, but there were still a good number left, and he thought that some of them might actually escape as they raced down the passage ahead of them. Suddenly, a chunk of the cobblestone wall disappeared in a cloud of dust and rubble as Digger and his pickaxe tore through the wall in front of the spiders. Pulling out his second pickaxe, he stepped into the spiders' midst, carving out great swaths of destruction. The villagers followed the big NPC, attacking the monster flank with Gameknight from the rear.

Knowing they were surrounded, the spiders now fought for hate's sake, their glowing red eyes focused on their enemy, Gameknight999. The NPCs quickly whittled down their numbers until only one remained. Surrounded and exhausted, the spider fell to the ground, fuzzy legs extended outward.

Crafter approached the creature cautiously, careful to stay out of range of those deadly claws.

"Why have you come here?" the young NPC asked.

The spider glared up at Crafter with disdain, then turned her eight bright red eyes toward Gameknight999.

"What is this about?" Gameknight asked as he stepped forward. "The Last Battle is over, and your Maker was destroyed."

"He wassss not desssstroyed," the spider said. "The Maker left the sssserver to torture the physss-sical world."

Gameknight looked at Crafter and smiled, then turned to the spider again.

"You have been lied to, spider," Gameknight said. "Herobrine was destroyed when he left the server. I destroyed him myself. He is not in the Minecraft servers and he is not in the physical world. He's gone."

"You lie!" the spider spat.

"Oh really?" Gameknight said. "Then why am I here if the physical world is being destroyed by Herobrine?"

"Well . . . you are . . . umm . . ." The fire in its eyes faded a bit as the spider considered this new information.

"The war is over," Gameknight said in a soft voice. "The time for peace is now. Herobrine has been deleted and his influence over the NPCs of the Overworld is done."

The spider looked up at the User-that-is-not-a-user and smiled an eerie, toothy smile.

"That issss what you think."

The spider launched herself at Gameknight999 in one final, desperate attack, her eight claws aimed right at his head. But before the creature could move more than half a block, arrows pierced the monster from all sides, taking the last of the spider's HP. She disappeared with a pop, leaving behind a handful of silk and three balls of glowing XP.

The User-that-is-not-a-user looked at Crafter, confused.

"What did she mean by that?" Gameknight asked.

"Who knows what any of these monsters mean?" Hunter said. "I'm just glad this attack is over. Now, let's finish the cobblestone roof over the village before any more spiders get bright ideas. If they all think Herobrine is still alive, they'll all be willing to risk their lives for him."

"She's right," Digger said as he headed back up the watchtower, the other NPCs following closely, blocks of cobblestone replacing weapons in their hands as they transitioned from angry warriors to peaceful villagers once again.

Crafter looked up at Gameknight, a concerned look in his blue eyes. He shook his head, confused.

"I guess we'll just have to wait and see what the spider meant," he said.

"I don't like that," the User-that-is-not-a-user replied. "I don't like that at all."

CHAPTER 6
VILLAGE IN PERIL

With guards watching the perimeter of the village, the NPCs worked hard to complete the cobblestone roof. As the stony cover grew, Gameknight and Crafter went through the village, placing torches on every wall, erasing the shadows and gloom the overhead layer of rock was giving the town.

"It's important to keep the light level up," Crafter said.

"Why?" Gameknight asked.

"Monsters like zombies and skeletons can spawn where the light level is low, which is why they usually spawn at night. But with this cover, the light level would always be low in the village, letting creatures appear at any time."

"That doesn't sound so good," Gameknight said.

"No, not at all," Crafter agreed.

So the companions ran through the village placing torches in every shadowy corner, driving away the darkness.

Finally, the new stone roof was complete and the village was protected from the bone and snowball downpour. Villagers went back to their normal work, replanting crops and tending to the livestock. Yes, there was a weird-looking cobblestone roof over everything, so things weren't exactly how they used to be, but Gameknight was starting to feel confident that the threat was over, at least for the moment.

A howling suddenly filled the air. Many of the villagers drew their swords, getting ready for another battle. But Gameknight recognized the sounds and put his hands up to indicate that they should lower their weapons, easing their fears.

"Don't worry. It is likely our companion, Herder, coming with some friends," he said.

As if on cue, Herder came through the village gates with a dozen wolves fast on his heels. He ran up to the village elders and stopped, his brow covered with sweat.

"These wolves will help protect the village," Herder said.

Gameknight beamed with pride.

"They will patrol the desert around the village and watch for monsters," Herder continued. "Listen for their howls. With all the bones here, you should have no difficulty keeping them happy. Take care of them and they will take care of you."

The largest of the wolves came forward and stood next to Herder. The lanky boy motioned for the wolf to approach the village's crafter. Moving silently, the creature approached the NPC cautiously, sniffing his outstretched hand, then wagged his tail and sat next to the village's leader. The other NPCs cheered as more of the wolves came forward to accept pats on the back from their new friends.

"Well done, Herder," Crafter said, smiling at the boy. Herder smiled back.

"It's time we made a plan," Hunters said as the cheering settled down.

"I think we should—" Stitcher started to say, but was interrupted by a villager bursting out of the watchtower.

"It's happened again! It's happened again," the NPC said as he skidded to a stop.

"What happened?" Gameknight asked.

"There's someone from the next village down in the crafting chamber," the NPC said. "Come quickly."

That was all the information he needed. Gameknight dashed for the door and shot through the tunnels. In seconds, he was at the crafting chamber door, where he saw, sitting on the ground next to a newly-arrived minecart, a villager. The color of her smock indicated she was a woodcutter, and the look on her pale face told a grim story. Taking the steps two at a time, the User-that-is-not-a-user sprinted to the newcomer. Behind him, he could hear others following close behind.

Gameknight slowed his pace and walked calmly across the crafting chamber floor, weaving around the numerous crafting benches and minecart tracks that covered the ground. Stepping to the NPC's side, he crouched.

"Is everything all right?" Gameknight asked.

The woodcutter looked up at him and instantly recognized who he was. She breathed a sigh of relief as color slowly started to seep back into her square face.

"They just fell all around the well!" Woodcutter cried. "We didn't know how it was happening or why. It's terrible."

"What is it?" Gameknight asked. "What's happening?"

She looked away from Gameknight and stared at the ground.

"It's terrible . . . their sound . . . awful . . . I can't get it out of my head."

She stopped talking as her shoulders slumped. She was so traumatized that she couldn't utter another word.

"We have to know what's going on," Gameknight said. "Where did she come from?"

"I know her," one of the NPCs in the chamber said. "She came from the next village on that track."

The villager pointed at the tunnel to his right.

"Come on," Gameknight said.

"Don't you think we should wait for—" Crafter started to ask, but he was cut off.

"No waiting," the User-that-is-not-a-user snapped. "Let's go!"

Gameknight placed a minecart on the tracks and pushed it forward into the dark tunnel. As the crafting chamber disappeared behind him, images of what *might be* started to fill his head. But one question began to cut through all the possibilities: *why was this happening now?*

CHAPTER 7

COMMAND BLOCKS

The constant, rhythmic clickity-clack of the minecart, coupled with the cool darkness of the tunnel, began to lull Gameknight999 to sleep. Images of Herobrine's bright, menacing eyes filled his mind as he relived every conflict, from that first encounter in front of Crafter's village to the terrible battle where Herder had been possessed in the Nether. In every one of the those battles, he'd had the chance to destroy that evil virus, but each time he'd fallen short and managed to let him escape, sometimes narrowly escaping his own death as well. If only he'd been able to stop him back then, they wouldn't be chasing his dangerous pranks across Minecraft now.

But they had, hadn't they? He was sure that they'd destroyed Herobrine once and for all. He would have been willing to bet his life on it. He'd been so sure before these weird pranks started happening through the Overworld. But these tricks were now making him doubt his convictions. Wouldn't it make sense that they were the work of

Herobrine, who had somehow still survived? Conflicting thoughts weighed heavily on Gameknight's mind as he whooshed through the tunnel.

His minecart burst into the bright light of the crafting chamber, and the User-that-is-not-a-user was instantly snapped awake. Pulling his minecart off the tracks, he set it in a nearby chest and waited for his friends. In a minute, they were all there, Hunter bringing up the rear.

Gameknight gazed around the chamber. He could see tools left lying on the ground as if they had been suddenly dropped. Half-finished chests sat hovering over crafting tables and dull, incomplete iron armor was scattered about nearby.

"It looks as if they left in a hurry," Digger said, his deep voice bouncing off the stone walls, coming back to them from all directions.

"I think it's best if we go up and see what happened for ourselves," Crafter suggested.

Gameknight nodded and led the way. Drawing his diamond sword, he charged up the steps and through the tunnels until he reached the cobblestone watchtower. But as he peered out the windows into the grassland village, he found everything looked . . . well, normal. There were patches of grass growing among blocks of sand, wooden homes sprinkled throughout the village, a tall cobblestone wall ringing the community. All of that looked as it should look. But what he could not see were any villagers.

"Where is everyone?" Stitcher asked.

"I don't know," Gameknight responded. "Let's go out and look around."

As soon as he opened the door, he heard a noise that he couldn't quite place. It was the sound of terrified animals screaming as loud as they could for a few moments, before being suddenly and immediately silenced.

"What was that?" Crafter asked, leaning out the door and looking around.

"It's sheep!" Herder cried as he shoved his way out of the watchtower and took off running to the left, toward the screams.

"Herder, wait!" Gameknight yelled, but there was no slowing down the lanky boy.

Sprinting as fast as he could, the User-that-is-not-a-user followed the young boy through the empty streets of the village. When he reached the end of the next building, he turned the corner, trying to stay fast on Herder's heels. He rounded the corner, expecting to still be far behind the boy. Instead, he nearly collided with him.

In front of Herder and Gameknight stood all the inhabitants of the village, motionless, in shocked silence. Beyond the crowd was the village's well. It was a cobblestone structure with a square roof on top, the source of water for the entire community. But right now, it was under attack.

"What's happening?" Gameknight asked in disbelief, looking up in the sky.

Sheep plummeted from the sky, landing on and around the well. The poor animals were bleating as they dropped, each one disappearing with a pop as soon as it landed.

It was beyond terrible.

Small cubes of wool floated just off the ground all around the structure, as well as some tools and armor. Gameknight scanned the crowd, looking for an NPC in a black smock. But all he could see were the square heads of the villagers, many of them looking down at the ground, weeping, unable to help the sheep. Gameknight continued scanning the crowd, and eventually saw flowing black hair resting against a black smock. It was the village's crafter.

"What's happening here?" the User-that-is-not-a-user asked as he approached.

"We don't know," the crafter replied with a defeated look on her face. She turned and looked at Gameknight with tears in her eyes.

"They just started falling from the sky," the crafter said, her voice cracking with emotion. "You can hear their cries of terror from high up in the air . . . oh . . . they must be so scared as they fall. How could anyone do such a thing?"

"Why didn't you build a pool of water to catch some of them?" Gameknight asked as he pushed through the crowd.

"We tried," the crafter answered.

"Builder and Carver tried," one of the NPCs said. "But each sheep is heavy, and when they're falling from such great heights they can be incredibly dangerous, and . . ."

The villager stopped speaking, overcome with emotion, and simply pointed to the collection of armor, tools, and weapons that floated among the cubes of wool. It was all that remained of the two volunteers.

"We have to do something," Herder cried, panic in his eyes. "I'll go out and—"

"No, Herder!" Gameknight snapped. "You'll do as I say." He turned back to the crafter. "I need buckets of water—now!"

The crafter looked at the User-that-is-not-a-user for a moment, trying to decipher what he might have in mind. Then, realizing that the village had tried everything they could already, to no avail, and hoping there was still a solution they hadn't thought of, she turned and looked at a group of villagers standing nearby.

"Well?" she asked. "Does anyone have water?"

Instantly, four full buckets were thrust toward him. Gameknight gestured to Herder, and the lanky boy collected them and put them safely in his inventory. Gameknight then pulled Herder close to his side and spoke softly in his ear.

"You stay close to me, as close as possible. Do you understand?"

Herder nodded.

Reaching out his right arm, he wrapped it around the boy and pulled him close. With his left, he pulled out his shield.

"Gameknight, what are you doing?" Digger asked from behind him.

"We're going to help those sheep," he replied.

"But there's too many," the stocky NPC said in protest. "Your shield can't take that kind of abuse."

The User-that-is-a-user moved forward anyway, ignoring the objections and holding his rectangular shield up over both his and Herder's heads. The first sheep that hit the shield almost tore it from his grasp. He wasn't prepared for the force of the blow. Gripping his only defense with all his strength, Gameknight continued on, slowly but steadily, holding Herder close.

"When we get close to the well, I want you to get under its roof," Gameknight shouted over the smashing animals and their terrified cries.

Herder looked up at his friend and nodded as he wiped tears from his eyes.

More sheep hammered his shield. At one point, two animals hit at the same time. His arm nearly buckled, but Gameknight's strength held. Their scared cries assailed him from all sides. They were now only four blocks from the well.

"Come on, Herder, let's go faster," the User-that-is-not-a-user said.

The pair increased their pace. When they reached the protective cover of the well's roof, both Herder and Gameknight jumped up onto the edge of the square structure. They could see the cool water down in the well and knew that if they fell into it, they would likely never be able to get out.

Carefully, Herder poured a bucket of water on the ground. It flowed outward in a six-block radius, creating a thin layer of water on the ground. But that layer was enough to cushion the fall of the bleating animals. Instead of being instantly killed, they survived. Herder moved precariously along the edge of the well to the next corner and emptied the next bucket of water out into the grass. As before, the sheep falling in that area survived. Gameknight watched as the fuzzy white creatures struggled out of the water, but once they escaped, they began to walk around the village as if nothing had happened.

Moving like a tightrope walker, Herder carefully made his way along the lip of the well until he reached the next corner. He poured the life-saving water onto the ground as before, and again, a circle of survival formed for the sheep, allowing the animals a chance to live. Moving to the fourth corner, he readied the last bucket, but was stopped.

"Herder, wait," Gameknight said as he moved up behind him. "There's a sign out there—I have to read it before the water washes it away. Wait until I tell you to place the water."

Herder nodded his boxy head, his long black hair hanging over his eyes.

Gameknight held the shield up over his head and stepped out into the bleating rain. The animals pounded on his shield when they struck. He could see small cracks starting to appear through the metal layer from the force of impact; he had to hurry. Scooting around the corner of the well, he stopped in front of the sign to read it quickly, then raced back to safety under the well's roof.

"Now . . . pour it!" Gameknight shouted over the din of the falling sheep.

Herder dumped the last bucket of water on the edge of the well. The pool of water quickly spread across the grass-covered ground. It uprooted the sign and pushed it aside as the thin blue coating of liquid expanded to a distance of six blocks.

Looking where the sign had been, Gameknight thought he saw a faint crimson glow, as if some kind of red light were buried under the ground. Gameknight started thinking.

"Herder, stay there," the User-that-is-not-a-user said.

Holding the shield over his head, he leapt off the well and ran outside the circle of woolly hail. The NPCs cheered for the User-that-is-not-a-user, but Gameknight ignored them. There was another mystery here; that red glow beneath the sign meant something, and he was going to find out what.

Putting away his shield, Gameknight pulled out a shovel and started digging. He carved steps into the ground three blocks deep, then dug straight toward the place where the sign had stood, leaving one block above him. Soon, he was enveloped in darkness as the entrance he had dug moved farther and farther behind him. But then a light flared behind him. Glancing over his shoulder, he found Crafter standing behind him, one torch placed in the wall and another in his hand.

"I don't know what you are doing, Gameknight999, but I'll help where I can."

The User-that-is-not-a-user gave his friend a nod, then turned and continued digging. He figured they were about six blocks from the red glow he'd seen. He could feel water drops falling on his head and shoulders; they were under one of Herder's protective pools. Glancing up, he could see cracks beginning to form in the blocks of dirt. The water was protecting the sheep's HP, but it was not stopping the impact from slowly destroying the blocks of dirt.

He had to move quickly.

Digging with all his strength, he closed the distance on his target. Removing two more blocks, he knew he was almost there. He dug up another pair of blocks, revealing a faint red glow that leaked from around the edges of the next block. When he removed the outlined block of dirt, Gameknight gasped in surprise.

"What do you see?" Crafter asked.

"Come look."

Crafter moved next to his friend, a look of shock on his face.

"What is it?" Crafter asked.

Before them was a hollowed-out chamber three blocks wide, a dozen long, and two blocks high. Glowing lines of redstone power zigzagged across the chamber, all of them connected in a complex series of repeaters and comparators, pulses of light moving through the structure like the beating of a heart. Directly under the location of the sign sat a block that Gameknight instantly recognized: a command block. But this one was different from others he'd used before. It was checkered orange, with what looked like blinking lights on the sides.

"It's a redstone timer circuit," Gameknight said. "And that strange block is called a command block. It must be what's causing the sheep to spawn up in the air."

"Redstone timer? Command block?" Crafter said, confused.

Gameknight ignored the question for the moment as he cleared another block of dirt from their path and stepped into the chamber. With a quick stroke of his shovel, he broke the redstone circuit, extinguishing the crimson light and plunging the chamber into darkness. Crafter pulled out a torch and placed it against the wall.

"You're telling me that this orange block was causing all those sheep to fall to their deaths?"

Gameknight nodded.

"And it was also messing with the cows and pigs? And the bone snow too? It was all because of command blocks?"

The User-that-is-not-a-user nodded again.

An angry scowl came across Crafter's face. Pulling an iron pickaxe out of his inventory, he swung it with all his strength, digging the metal point into the checkered block. The tool bounced off it harmlessly, as if he were trying to mine diamond with a wooden shovel. He swung again. The iron tool ricocheted off the unblemished block, small iron chips breaking off the tool and spraying both of them.

"You can't break them," Gameknight said. "They're as indestructible as bedrock."

"How do we destroy it?" Crafter asked.

"We have to destroy the redstone power source, which we just did." Gameknight put a hand on the NPC's pick and carefully pushed it down. "I assure you, it's dead."

Crafter gave a sigh of relief.

"What did the sign say?"

Now it was Gameknight's turn to sigh.

"It said 'THIS IS BECAUSE OF GAME-KNIGHT999. PREPARE FOR RETRIBUTION. SEE YOU IN THE NEXT VILLAGE.' And it was signed '—HEROBRINE.'"

Gameknight looked down into Crafter's bright blue eyes as a shudder ran down his spine. *How can this be?* he thought. *Is that virus still in Minecraft? Is Herobrine still alive?*

All the villagers say they can feel Herobrine is gone from the servers, but how can that be true while these signs and command blocks keep popping up? His doubt about Herobrine's fate began to chip away at his own confidence. *Maybe I am responsible?*

"Is this all my fault?" he asked his friend, his voice barely a whisper.

"Of course not," Crafter snapped. "But we must tell the others. Now that we've figured out the command blocks, we can help the other communities. Come on!"

CHAPTER 8

REAPER

The skeleton king rode majestically atop his bony horse, a crown of bones leaning slightly to one side on top of his pale skull. Behind him marched a hundred of his best fighters, all of them expert archers and experienced warriors. Reaper dismounted when they reached the mouth of the tunnels and handed the skeleton horse's reins off to one of his subordinates.

"Which way now?" he asked the large black spider that stood at his side.

"The chamber issss thissss way," the spider hissed.

Moving quickly, the spider scurried into the tunnel, her red eyes seeming to glow brighter in the darkness, with the army of skeletons fast on her eight heels. She led them through so many twists and turns that at first it seemed like it would have been impossible to get back out without her.

I got lost when they led me out of that chamber to collect my troops, Reaper thought. *Is this spider trying to purposely confuse us and make it impossible to ever leave this place? What kind of game is Shaivalak playing?*

But then he noticed the blocks of spiderweb placed high up on the walls, carefully positioned in the shadows so as not to be easily noticed. They were markers, showing the spider where to go. Reaper continued to follow the dark monster through the twisting passages, descending deeper into the bowels of Minecraft, keeping an eye on the position of the markers. Soon, they passed a section of tunnel with a large opening in the side. Pausing, the skeleton king gazed through the opening and down into a massive chamber lit with a scant few redstone torches. He could see the narrow bridge stretching from the cavern entrance. The single-block-wide crossing led to a large cobblestone platform that appeared to float in the middle of the cavern, only touching the walls at a few strategic places. Beneath the platform, all he could see was darkness, the cavern stretching far below into the shadows. Another bridge extended away from the cobblestone platform, but whatever it led to was shrouded in darkness. Blocks of some kind were barely visible, but Reaper could not tell what they were.

"That issss Herobrine'ssss cave," the spider hissed.

"I know that, spider," Reaper snapped. "I've been here before. Just lead on."

Without a reply, the spider moved off, continuing through the sloping passage. In minutes, they were at the cavern entrance.

"My queen hassss ordered that the sssskeletonsss are to guard thissss entrance with their livessss, and refusssse entrance to any usssser or NPC," the spider said.

"You don't give commands here, spider," the king of the skeletons growled. "Leave us."

The eight-legged creature glared up at the bony monster, then turned and scuttled back through the tunnels, likely heading for the surface.

Pulling out his massive longbow made of pale white bone, Reaper strode across the narrow bridge, unconcerned about the lethal drop that yawned on either side, and stepped onto the large platform. Moving to the edge of the bridge, but nervous about following their king across the narrow walkway, many of the skeleton warriors peered over the edge, down into the darkness. Reaper drew an arrow out of his inventory and dropped it over the side. The silence seemed to go on forever, and with each passing second, the skeletons grew more and more uncomfortable. Finally, it hit the ground with a tiny *plink*.

"Hmm. It must be a great distance down to the bottom," the skeleton king said to no one in particular.

"Yesss, farther than you can imagine," a voice replied from behind him.

Spinning around, Reaper drew another arrow from his inventory, notched it to his bowstring, and drew it back all in one fluid motion. Before him was the spider queen, Shaivalak. He recognized her by the purple eyes that peered up at him.

"We have done as Herobrine asked," Reaper said, lowering his bow. "Here are a hundred of my finest warriors. We are ready to battle the User-that-is-not-a-user."

"Excellent," Shaivalak said. "Guard thissss chamber well, for Gameknight999 hassss already been sssspotted. Herobrine sssseekssss to have hissss revenge on the Usssser-that-is-not-a-usssser and all the NPCssss of the Overworld. On the far platform issss hissss greatessst invention. It will dessssstroy all of the NPC villagessss and Gameknight999 will be forced to watch."

The spider queen moved across the platform to the other single-block-wide bridge, which stretched into darkness, the other side hidden from sight. Reaper followed close behind. He hadn't looked closely at the blocks that last time he was here, and now he was curious.

As they drew closer, Reaper could just barely make out the strange blocks in the shadows. There were lines on the ground connecting them all together. On the far side of the platform, he could see a hole in the cavern wall. Bright orange lava flowed out of the opening and fell into a large pool below. High up on the wall of the cavern was a display that showed the number 82 . . . tick . . . no, it was now 81.

"Gameknight999 will be here ssssoon," Shaivalak said. "The Maker hassss predicted it."

"The Maker predicted it, you say?" the skeleton king asked.

The spider did not reply.

"I just wish Herobrine could have left a portion of his code in the server," Reaper said. "It would be a treat to see the Maker's delight when the villagers are all destroyed."

"The Maker decidessss hissss path," the spider queen said. "We cannot quesssstion hissss plan.

He issss gone, wreaking vengeance on the physss-sical world, and we are here to carry out hissss lasssst commandsssss."

The king of the skeletons grunted, as if uncon-cerned, then glanced up at the ticking clock and smiled. Looking around the platform, he consid-ered possible defenses against the User-that-is-not-a-user. There was no place for his warriors to hide and shoot their bows. They'd have to stand out in the open and fire—not ideal, but his warriors could easily cover that narrow bridge that led to the cobblestone platform.

"We will do what we must, but I have learned to not underestimate the User-that-is-not-a-user," Reaper said. "What if he comes here with more vil-lagers than I have skeletons?"

The spider queen moved across the platform to a strange-looking block at the edge of the stony plane. In the dim light, he could see that it was checkered, with an orange tint to it. Next to the block was a lever in the "OFF" position.

"The Maker left ussss thissss block jusssst for Gameknight999," Shaivalak said. "If he getssss by your sssskeletonssss, then he will have to deal with all of the sssspidersssss thissss block will ssssummon. Hundredssss of the sssssistersss will be sssspawned if I flip thissss lever. Our enemiessss do not sssstand a chance."

Reaper nodded, appreciating the deviousness of the plan. If Gameknight was able to get past the spiders out in the Overworld, and get past his skel-etons, then the spider queen would summon hun-dreds of her minions to finish off what was left of the User-that-is-not-a-user and his friends. Their victory was guaranteed.

The skeleton king leaned his head back and laughed a dry, hacking laugh that echoed off the rocky walls.

"Perfect!" Reaper said as he looked down at his fuzzy ally.

And as he stared at her, Shaivalak's eyes began to glow bright purple with evil intent.

CHAPTER 9

FANGS AND FUR

They emerged from the tunnels and into the crafting chamber of the next village. Gameknight was the first to leap out of his minecart. Drawing his diamond sword, he scanned the room for threats. The NPCs working in front of crafting tables stared at the User-that-is-not-a-user with quizzical looks on the faces.

Then Digger was at his side, two pickaxes held at the ready. He, too, surveyed his surroundings, knowing that another trap could be waiting for them, but lowered his huge tools when he saw they were safe.

"Herobrine's command block must be somewhere up on the surface," Gameknight said.

Glancing over his shoulder, he saw the rest of his friends had emerged from the tunnel.

"Come on, everyone," Gameknight shouted. "To the surface!"

The User-that-is-not-a-user charged up the steps that led out of the crafting chamber. Surging through the iron doors at the top of the stairs, he sped through the tunnels that would take him to the secret entrance in the watchtower.

As he ran through the subterranean passages, Gameknight could hear the footsteps of his friends behind him. He was glad they were there. The last sign supposedly left behind by Herobrine made him wonder if all this suffering really was his fault. Had he, by battling with Herobrine, brought all the pain and death to the NPCs of the Overworld? Images of those who had perished came to his mind: Baker, Weaver, Stonecutter, Builder, Tiller, the Woodcutter twins . . . the list was endless, and they all had suffered because of his war with Herobrine. Had he been the cause? Feelings of uncertainty circled his soul like a predatory cat, getting ready to strike.

Without realizing it, Gameknight had climbed the tall ladder and emerged in the watchtower. He moved quickly to the door and looked out the inset window.

What he saw made him shake this head in disbelief.

Villagers were going about their normal lives in this grassland village. They were tending crops, caring for livestock, repairing tools, everything you'd think a village would be doing when it was at peace.

Gameknight opened the door and burst out into the courtyard, his diamond blade held at the ready. Scanning the area, he quickly realized there was something strange about this village, but he couldn't quite figure out what.

"You notice it?" Crafter asked.

"What are you talking about?" Gameknight replied, his eyes darting from left to right, looking for threats.

"No walls," Crafter said, a perplexed smile on his face.

Turning in a circle, Gameknight finally realized what had seemed off: there were no fortifications of any kind around the cluster of buildings. The village had been built on a small swath of grassland completely surrounded by a mega taiga biome. The incredibly tall spruces and gentle leafy ferns formed a protective cocoon that kept the village from view, acting a bit like a natural wall. This town, Gameknight realized, was a little hidden pocket of peace within the server.

"It's likely the monsters don't even know about this village," Crafter said.

Gameknight nodded, then smiled.

"That's exactly correct," said the village's crafter as he approached. He glanced at Gameknight999, and his diamond armor and sword, and scowled. "And that's the way we like it as well."

He walked forward to face the visitors.

"I'm this village's crafter, as you can see by my clothing. We have managed to avoid all of the trouble that has been brewing across the server because of our unique location in the middle of this mega taiga biome," the crafter said, gesturing to their surroundings. "We have no arguments with the monsters of the Overworld, and they leave us alone. So I mean no disrespect when I ask, what do you want here?"

"There is reason to believe that your village will be attacked," Gameknight said.

"That seems unlikely," the crafter said. "Just what do you believe will be attacking us?"

"Well . . . we don't know for sure," Gameknight replied, embarrassed.

Hunter giggled, then grunted when Stitcher punched her in the arm.

Herder stepped forward, moving past the village's crafter, then paused and stood still.

"You hear them?" he said, casting a smile at Gameknight.

"Hear what?" the User-that-is-not-a-user replied.

"Friends!" the lanky boy said excitedly.

Just then, the faintest of howls could be heard drifting out of the forest: wolves. They sounded full of strength and pride. Long ago, the wolves had been brought into Minecraft by the Oracle. She was an anti-virus program that had been added to Minecraft to combat Herobrine and his monsters. In an attempt to battle the Maker, the Oracle had crafted the wolves, using them as her personal army of hunters that pursued Herobrine across the server. They were added in the Beta version, long before Gameknight ever transported into the game, but after the Great Zombie Invasion of the old, pre-Alpha days, when the awakening of Minecraft had first occurred.

The wolves were staunch allies and friends to Herder. He had an uncanny way of communicating with them, the furry creatures always willing to do his bidding. Reaching into his inventory, Herder pulled out a handful of bones and looked longingly into the forest.

"You should wait," Gameknight said, seeing the expression on his friend's face. "There's a trap somewhere nearby. Herobrine has some command blocks buried in this village, but they aren't working yet. We should stay together until we know what might happen when they are activated."

The howls became louder as the wolves approached the village from all sides. By now, the NPCs had all come out of their homes and congregated with the newcomers at the center of their village, faces filled with welcoming smiles. They looked excited at the sounds of the animals in the forest, many of them holding bones in their blocky hands; treats for the unexpected guests. Gameknight imagined the creatures smelling the bones that awaited them and zipping around the spruces and ferns of the taiga, their fur making them look like bolts of white lightning.

But then the sound of the wolves grew strange. The majestic howls changed to angry growls. In the distance, Gameknight saw a large group of the animals skid to a stop just at the tree line of the shadowy forest, their white fur standing out against the dark shadows.

"What are they doing?" Herder asked, frowning. "Why aren't they coming into the village?"

Gameknight squinted, straining to see the animals more clearly. Strangely, he realized that the wolves' eyes were bright red. They growled and bared their teeth. The wolves were hostile for some reason, the User-that-is-not-a-user realized, and it made no sense that they would be acting like this.

The snarling creatures walked slowly out of the forest and toward the village, their sharp teeth showing behind drawn lips, eyes like bright pinpoints of crimson fire.

"Everyone back up slowly," Gameknight said as he drew his sword. "There's something wrong with these wolves. They're angry for some reason."

"The wolves have always been our friends," one of the villagers said, ignoring the warning as he ran out to meet them, a bone in each hand. When he reached the animals, they fell on him, a dozen wolves attacking all at once.

"NOOOO!" Herder screamed.

Gameknight wanted to go out and help the NPC, but he knew the villager didn't have a chance. In seconds, he was gone.

"What's happening?" Crafter said.

"I don't know," Gameknight replied. "Everyone be careful!"

The creatures came even closer. Turning in a circle, Gameknight could see the wolves had the village completely surrounded. There were probably a hundred of them, all red-eyed, their fur bristling with anger.

"It's Herobrine," Hunter said. "He's doing this, somehow."

"We have to find the control blocks, fast, or the village will be wiped out!" Crafter cried.

"Run for the crafting chamber!" one of the villagers cried.

"No, stand still!" Herder screamed. "They will attack anyone that moves. Stay perfectly still."

But the NPC that yelled didn't listen. He ran for the watchtower, a look of fear on his face as he sped away, trying to outrun the dangerous beasts. But instantly, ten wolves shot out of formation and fell on the fleeing villager. As before, the doomed NPC disappeared in seconds, the wolves destroying the villager's HP. Then they turned and faced Gameknight999.

Drawing his second sword, Gameknight scanned the village for the sign that he knew would be there.

"I see it," Digger said, having the same thought. "Over there."

He pointed with his big pickaxe. Gameknight turned and saw a sign standing next to the blacksmith's shop.

"That must be where the command blocks are buried," Gameknight said. "Herder, take out your shovel. Your job is to dig up the dirt and break the redstone circuit."

"What do the rest of us do?" Crafter asked.

"Protect Herder," Gameknight answered. "It's the command blocks that are making the wolves angry, I'm sure of it. We need to cut the power to those blocks so that we can save this village from complete annihilation. Everyone ready?" They nodded. "OK . . . RUN!"

The group sprinted for the blacksmith's shop, weapons held at the ready. The wolves instantly responded, charging toward the party. Angry growls filled the air as the wolves streaked toward them. Gameknight was the first to reach the shop. Turning, he saw a wolf closing on Stitcher. Dropping his sword, he pulled out his bow and fired, sadness filling his soul. His enchanted arrow instantly burst into flames as it leapt from his bow and streaked through the air. When it struck the wolf, the furry creature yelped in pain as the flaming arrow tore into its HP, forcing the animal to abandon its attack and veer away. Gameknight's heart broke at the sound of that animal's yelping, but he couldn't let it hurt his friend.

Picking up his sword, he charged forward, swinging it before him. The others reached the blacksmith's shop and formed a protective circle around Herder, who was already digging feverously. A wolf shot forward and snapped at Gameknight's leg, its sharp teeth carving deep marks into his leggings.

Striking with his diamond sword, he hit the wolf with the flat edge of the blade. The animal growled, then bit him again, scoring another hit.

"Hurry, Herder!" Gameknight screamed as he kicked at the animal. "I don't want to hurt the wolves, but soon we won't have much choice."

The wolf lunged at him again, but suddenly, Digger's big pickaxe hit the creature, the side of the tool sending the animal flying. Before Gameknight could thank his friend, two more wolves attacked. They leapt up at him, sharp teeth bared. Without any other option, Gameknight brought up his diamond sword and slashed at the majestic animals. The attacking pair yelped in pain as his blade bit into their HP, making them flash red.

"I'm so sorry," Gameknight said, but the animals turned and attacked again. This time, he drew his iron sword, which would cause less damage, and swung it at the two wolves, tearing more HP from their furry bodies. They yelped in pain and backed off, glaring up at Gameknight, their eyes burning bright red with hatred. Crouching, they readied another attack, but Gameknight knew that they could not survive another hit from his sword.

"Please don't," Gameknight begged. "I don't want to hurt you."

He took a step back as the two wolves advanced.

"Hurry, Herder," he said, pleading. "HURRY!"

The two wolves growled, crouched even lower, then sprang into the air, their fanged mouths aimed directly for Gameknight999.

CHAPTER 10

BLAME

Herder cried out, "I found it!"

There was a loud, cracking sound as the young boy destroyed the redstone circuit, turning off the command blocks. The wolves instantly stopped their growling. The eyes of the two wolves flying through the air went from violent red to peaceful black as their bristling fur fell back against their bodies, their tails sagging. Gameknight dropped his swords and caught the two animals in midair, then fell back as they landed in a heap. Herder was there almost immediately with bones, quickly taming the animals.

As Gameknight stood up, he pulled out a steak and gave one to each wolf, allowing their HP to regenerate. He then reached down and petted each one of them.

"Is everyone OK?" Gameknight asked, wiping sweat from his brow.

He glanced around at his companions and could see that they were all still standing, though many looked like they'd taken damage.

"How could this happen?" the village crafter cried. "The wolves have never attacked us before!"

Gameknight spun around and saw the villager sitting on the ground near the items of those that had lost their lives.

"They've always been our friends," he said as he wiped tears from his eyes.

"They're still your friends," Herder snapped. "This was Herobrine's doing. He warped the minds of the wolves with his command blocks."

The crafter stood and collected the items, then moved to the sign that stood next to the blacksmith's shop. Gameknight walked to his side and looked at the sign.

"What does it say?" Stitcher asked.

"It says, 'THIS ONE IS THE FIRST OF MANY,'" Gameknight read.

"There's another message on the back of the building!" Digger yelled from the other side of the shop. The NPC carefully dug around the bottom of the sign to see if there were more command blocks lying in wait. The stocky NPC breathed a sigh of relief when he saw there were none.

"What does it say?" Gameknight asked, afraid that he might already know.

Digger looked up at the sign and read the words silently. When he finished, his face took on a worried look as he stepped away. He looked at Gameknight with concern in his eyes.

"What is it?" Gameknight asked. "What does it say?"

Digger just looked back with compassion in his eyes. Gameknight feared the worst. Moving to the side of the building, he looked up at the sign.

Digger spoke in a sad voice. "It says, 'ALL THIS IS GAMEKNIGHT'S FAULT. HE SHOULD HAVE SURRENDERED EARLIER.' It's signed '—HEROBRINE.'"

Gameknight stepped away from the sign and sighed.

This is a nightmare! he thought. *If I had figured out a way to defeat Herobrine earlier, would the people who were suffering be safe now?*

His train of thought was derailed as Digger's pick tore into the sign with a loud *crack!* and it splintered into a million pieces.

"This isn't your fault," Crafter said. "This is Herobrine's doing and is not your responsibility. I won't let that evil virus make me think otherwise."

"But what if I'd brought my dad into this sooner instead of hiding it from him? Maybe we'd have captured Herobrine sooner," Gameknight said quietly, looking down at the ground.

"You don't know that!" Hunter snapped. "Who knows how things would have played out if things had been done differently? Maybe things would have come out worse. Maybe he would have won. We don't know. But you don't get to take all this guilt onto yourself."

"But if—" Gameknight tried to continue, but was interrupted.

"There is no *if,* there is just *now,*" Hunter snapped. "And right now, we need to figure out where the next attack might be, and get there before any villagers are hurt."

"Agreed," Crafter said.

Gameknight sighed as he saw the determined looks on his friends' faces. They were all so confident that they could solve this problem. He wished he had that same hope. How could they possibly know where the next incident would occur?

"Let's get to the crafting chamber, then we'll figure out which way we need to go," Crafter said.

But before any of them could move, villagers streamed from the watchtower, each of them dripping wet.

"What's going on?" Hunter asked.

One of the villagers ran to her, then stopped to catch his breath. He was completely soaked, and Gameknight could see his HP was dangerously low. Reaching into his inventory, he handed the NPC a loaf of bread. The villager quickly ate the loaf, then nodded at Gameknight, thanking him.

"What happened?" Crafter asked.

"The crafting chamber is flooded," the NPC said. "Water is pouring in from all the tunnels, and the chamber is underwater. We tried to find the water source and block it off, but it seems like there's more than one. We've contained the water, but the tunnels are useless. We don't know how far the water extends along the minecart tunnels, and the rails are destroyed. If anyone uses the minecart network here, they might drown."

"It seems we still dance to Herobrine's tune," Crafter said, grimacing. "He clearly doesn't want us using the minecart network."

"Then we proceed on foot," Digger said, hefting his big pickaxe over his shoulder. "But what direction do we choose?"

"Which way is the nearest village?" Crafter asked the soaked NPC.

"That way, through the taiga and then through the mesa," the villager said, pointing to the northeast.

"OK then, we have a direction. Let's get moving," Crafter said.

"Everyone gather the supplies that you'll need," Digger said.

"Herder, I think it's best if you leave all these wolves here with this village," Crafter said to the lanky NPC. "They're going to need the creatures' protection until they can build a wall around their community."

Crafter looked at the villagers with his aged, bright-blue eyes. "You have gone unnoticed until now. But the monsters likely know of your presence and will be here soon. A wall is your only hope of survival. I'm sorry we cannot stay and help, but I fear we have bigger problems to deal with."

Stitcher then stepped forward and spoke in a low voice. "We should take some of the wolves with us for our own protection. I think the monsters of the Overworld will have their eyes on us as well."

"You are probably right," Crafter said, then nodded to Herder.

The boy pulled out bones from his inventory, then ran through the crowd of wolves, taming each one with a tap of the bone. Soon, the entire massive pack wore brown collars around their necks. Pulling a dozen aside, he knelt down and whispered into their ears, giving each one a separate command. Then he stood up to face the rest of the animals.

"Protect," Herder said in a clear voice.

The wolves barked, then some spread out around the village while others shot into the woods, looking for threats. The dozen he'd spoken to stayed at his side. He turned and smiled at Crafter, his grin reaching his sparkling, two-color eyes.

"Everyone gather supplies," Gameknight said. "We don't know when we'll get to the next village; we must be prepared."

The party spread out, asking the villagers for what they needed, while the village crafter repaired armor and weapons for Gameknight and his friends. Standing on the edge of the village, the User-that-is-not-a-user gazed into the dark spruce forest that encircled the village. For some reason, he felt as if the forest were staring back at him. Was he going crazy?

"You can't let Herobrine's words get to you," Crafter said. "He's lying to make you upset."

"But—"

Crafter held up a hand, silencing his friend.

"Don't play his game," Crafter said. "If you start to blame yourself, then you're doing exactly what he wants. Do you think that is the best thing to do?"

"No," Gameknight replied, his head hung in shame.

"That's right. So maybe you should hold your head up and be confident. You're the User-that-is-not-a-user, the person that defeated Herobrine and ended his reign of terror. Stand up straight!"

Gameknight reluctantly pulled his head up and stood tall.

"That's better," Crafter said. "Now, go get some supplies. We should leave by noon."

Gameknight gave his friend a smile, then went to a villager to get food and torches . . . and, of course, TNT.

The spider that lurked high overhead, nestled amid the branches of a tall spruce, wanted to laugh at the foolish NPCs, but knew remaining hidden for now was more important. She watched as the villagers scurried about, collecting items for their quest . . . how pathetic. Closing her multiple red eyes, she sent her thoughts to the queen of the spiders, then waited to receive new instructions. Being a direct descendant of Shaivalak, she had this particular ability to communicate, her thoughts merging into those of her queen and the rest of the queen's descendants. The sister gave a sinister smile when she heard Shaivalak's plans unfold within her spidery mind. The monster's eyes glowed bright red at the thought of her sisters destroying the terrible User-that-is-not-a-user. She resisted the urge to click her mandibles together with evil glee, then burrowed deeper into the branches of the spruce, staying out of sight . . . and waiting.

CHAPTER 11

BRYCE

They left the village with the sun at its zenith, the noonday light streaming through the high overhead tree branches, creating islands of bright illumination within the sea of shadows that covered the forest floor. With the bright patches of light, it was unlikely they would run into any zombies or skeletons, but even so, they kept a watchful eye on their surroundings. Herder's wolves formed a protective ring around the companions and made them all feel a bit safer.

Digger led them northeast, toward the nearest village that sat far in the distance. According to the last village's crafter, they could make it there just before dusk, but they had to hurry.

"You got a weird feeling being in these woods?" Gameknight asked Hunter.

She turned and looked at him, her enchanted bow casting an iridescent purple glow on the nearby trees.

"Yeah . . . like we're being watched," Hunter whispered.

Gameknight nodded, then glanced up at the treetops. He'd been scanning the dark green leaves since they left, and every once in a while he swore he saw something move, but sometimes a breeze moved the high branches and made it look like something was up there watching them. Then again, it would be easy for something to hide up there and remain unseen.

"Let's move faster," Gameknight said in a low voice.

They shifted from walking to running, trying to move as quietly as the wolves, which was impossible.

Soon they reached the edge of the forest. Gameknight stopped and sat down to catch his breath. Before him stretched a strange landscape filled with bands of brown, tan, beige, and mustard-yellow colors, all stratified into layers that stretched out across the plateaus. Narrow valleys revealed layers of colors within their steep sides. It reminded Gameknight of the sand sculpture he'd done one year at summer camp. They'd poured different colored sand into a vase, one color atop another, creating vibrant layers within the glass container. That was how this land looked.

Just beyond the mesas was a collection of narrow, colorful mountains. They weren't very tall, but they were incredibly steep. Around their bases ran a complex network of shallow chasms only ten to twelve blocks deep, but with walls that were nearly vertical and impossible to climb. Gameknight knew this to be the Bryce biome, named after Bryce Canyon National Park in Utah. It was beautiful.

"The NPCs said the next village will be on the other side of this biome," Crafter said. "It must be past all those brown spires."

"That's the Bryce biome," Gameknight said.

"I've never seen it before," Crafter said.

"It's fantastic," Digger said, the big NPC's blue-green eyes wide with amazement.

"We should get moving," Stitcher said.

"Yeah, let's get the sightseeing over with," Hunter added. "I don't want to be out there in all those chasms after dark. We'll never be able to see the monsters coming until it's too late."

"Agreed," Gameknight said. "Let's go."

He went forward, splashing through a narrow stream that separated the mega taiga from the brown mesa. Herder's wolves darted past him. The furry creatures shot through the water at incredible speed, then raced up the sloped landscape to the top of the mesa. Gameknight was always amazed at how fast they could run. Turning, he looked back at Herder and found the lanky boy smiling, pride showing on his square face.

"Let's get up on top of the mesa and find an easy path across this land," Crafter suggested.

Gameknight nodded and climbed the gradual incline that led to the top of a plateau. The land was completely flat across the summit, the ground underfoot a chocolate brown. In fact, all of the land around him was the same color. The brown land-scape stretched out in all directions with multiple valleys carved through the seemingly endless plain. The valleys curved to the left and right, taking cir-cuitous routes through the landscape. Gameknight knew following those valleys would add hours to their journey, which they couldn't afford. For now, they had to stay on top of the mesa so as to get to the next village as soon as possible.

"Northeast is this way," Digger said as he started walking.

"We run!" Hunter said as she sprinted by him.

The rest of the party raced to follow her example. At times, they had to run down the side of a narrow valley, only to climb the other side and continue their sprint to the northeast. As he ran, Gameknight turned his head, scanning their surroundings and looking for threats. He didn't like being on top of the mesa and out in the open; it was flat and empty and there was no place to hide. Monsters would be able to see them from far away, and with the dark landscape surrounding them, the creatures of the night would be difficult to spot.

"Gameknight," Crafter said, moving up next to him.

"What?"

"Spiders."

"Where?" he asked.

Crafter gestured over his right shoulder.

The User-that-is-not-a-user looked in that direction, trying not to be conspicuous. Far to the right, he could see a cluster of spiders. It looked like the group was at least twenty strong, if not more.

"Yeah, I saw them too, a few moments ago," Stitcher said. "They just popped up over the ridge on the left."

"On the left . . . what are you talking about?" Gameknight asked.

Looking to the left, he gasped.

"They're on both sides of us," Digger said as he pulled out his pickaxe.

Gameknight glanced to the left and right and sighed. There were far too many for them to fight. Even with Herder's wolves, they would be outnumbered and overrun. They could not stand and confront the dark monsters. They had only one option.

"What do we do?" Crafter asked.

"We run," Gameknight said.

"We can't run from spiders," Herder said. "They're faster than us. My wolves might be able to slow them down for a bit, but not for long."

"Gameknight, what do we do?" Crafter asked, his blue eyes filled with fear.

Gameknight glanced around. Everything was flat, with no place to hide. But then he remembered what lay ahead in the Bryce biome: a labyrinth of narrow chasms weaving their way around tall spires of multicolored clay. They could lose them in the maze.

"Follow me," Gameknight said. "We'll lose the spiders in all the twisting passages and chasms."

"I hope you know what you're doing," Digger said.

"Since when did that ever stop him before?" Hunter replied with a smile.

The companions ran into the winding passages that cut through the landscape. Tall spires of brown and tan and pale yellow clay loomed high into the air around them, the earthy spikes casting long shadows across the chasm as the sun raced to the horizon.

"If we get stuck out here after dark, we'll get lost," Crafter said. "We have to keep heading northeast whenever possible."

"Just keep your eye on the sun," Gameknight said as he led the company into a narrow curving passage. The sandy walls hugged them close; at times, the passage was only a single block wide.

"Herder, have the wolves take up a rear guard position," Gameknight said.

The lanky boy nodded, then whistled, calling the animals. In seconds, he had a dozen wolves running at his side.

"Protect behind," Herder said to the largest animal in the pack.

Somehow, the creature understood and slowed, allowing the rest of the group to pull away.

Their path now started to wind back and forth, carving wide, twisting passageways through the multihued clay. It was sometimes difficult to tell where they were heading, but Crafter seemed confident they were still going in the right direction.

They had been on the move for a little while when they all heard the unmistakable clicking of spiders high overhead.

"Everyone hide," Gameknight said in a whisper.

Quickly, he dug a hole in the ground two blocks deep and jumped in it, the others doing the same. Herder's wolves caught up with the group, and all surrounded the boy, their white fur standing out against the rusty sand.

If the spiders see the wolves, we're done for, Gameknight thought.

"Herder, send the wolves away," the User-that-is-not-a-user whispered. "They're too easy to see."

The young NPC gave his friend a sad look, then nodded. Whispering into the ear of the alpha male, he sent the wolves back toward the mega taiga.

"Hopefully, they will lead some of the spiders away," Herder whispered. "They'll find us later."

"If there *is* a later," Hunter mumbled.

Without warning, a group of spiders flowed over the edge of the chasm. With little effort, they scaled the steep walls and charged. Climbing out of their holes, the NPCs had no choice but to draw their weapons and attack. Gameknight was grateful when he counted only six monsters; it could have been a lot worse. Charging, he ran straight through the mob with his shield out, using it like a snow-plow. The spiders tumbled aside, allowing him to streak by. When he reached the end, he turned and fell on the back ranks with his sword drawn while the rest of the company attacked the front, trapping the spiders from both sides.

A spider charged at him, slashing with its dark claws. Gameknight blocked the attack with his shield, then swung at the monster with his diamond sword. The creature flashed red, then attacked again. Claw met diamond as he brought his sword up, but a second claw curved around from the other side and found his chest plate. Fortunately, his armor protected him. Turning, he dropped the shield and drew his iron sword. Spinning like a mad, razor-sharp top, he dove into the spider formations, slashing and hitting everything within reach. As he fought, flaming arrows streaked through the air, hitting the monsters near him. In seconds, it was over.

Bending down, Gameknight picked up his shield.

"Why did they attack with only six spiders?" Herder asked.

"They split up their forces to find us," Gameknight said. "Exactly what I hoped they would do."

"But that means there are still more creatures out there looking for us," Crafter said.

"Yeah, and we need them to go to the wrong place," the User-that-is-not-a-user said. "Crafter, do you have any of your fireworks with you?"

"Of course," the NPC replied. "My great-great-uncle . . ."

"Please, not now," Hunter said, rolling her eyes.

Crafter stopped, looking embarrassed, then pulled the red-and-white striped rocket from his inventory.

"Hook it up to a tripwire," Gameknight said. "If the fireworks go off, we'll know that more spiders have gotten onto our trail, and it will give us a little more warning."

"Set it up and let's keep going," Digger said. "The sun is getting lower."

Crafter set up the trap, then started running, following Digger and Hunter through the twisting pathway. Only a few minutes later, an explosion erupted high overhead. The green, sparkling face of a creeper looked down upon them as they followed the curving pathway.

"Everyone, sprint!" Digger said.

As they ran, the chasm straightened out and they could see the end of the biome. Just past the Bryce were rolling grassy hills; a grassland biome.

"Come on!" Gameknight said.

But a clicking sound, like a thousand crickets, filled the air ahead. A wave of spiders filed into the end of the chasm, blocking their exit to the grasslands. In the dimming light of dusk, the bright red eyes of the spiders looked like hateful, burning coals, all of them focused on their prey.

"What do we do?" Stitcher asked, her voice shaking.

The spiders behind them hadn't closed in on them yet, but Gameknight was sure that the loud clicking of the spiders would carry through the curving passes and alert the monsters pursuing them from the rear. Soon, the other half of the spider army would be on them.

"Gameknight, what do we do?" Stitcher asked.

"Maybe we should turn around and run for it," Digger said, his voice edged with fear.

"What if we climb the walls of the chasm?" Crafter suggested, his voice on the verge of panic.

"What do we do? Gameknight, tell us—save us—"

But the User-that-is-not-a-user could not come up with a single idea. He realized now that he had led his friends to this point, and their deaths would be his fault, just like the fate of the villages from Herobrine's command blocks. Herobrine's mocking signs had him doubting whether he could be trusted to lead anyone to safety again. As the spiders closed in, he understood that in trying to help, he'd just made everything worse. Around him, his friends were panicking, yelling out ideas they all knew would never work. This was the end, and all Gameknight could do was stand there, consumed with terror, as the spiders started clicking faster and faster, then finally charged forward, a black fuzzy wave of death flowing through the narrow chasm.

CHAPTER 12

TRAPPED

A loud voice rang out from behind the spiders in front of the group, causing the monsters to stop and turn around. Before they had time to move, the thundering sound of hooves filled the chasm like an impending storm. A chorus of battle cries replied to the first voice as the hoofbeats became louder. And then what seemed to Gameknight like the most beautiful thing in the world happened. Heavily armed cavalry smashed through the spider formation, crushing the monsters under the weight of their warhorses. They drove through the spiders and kept going, charging up to Gameknight and his friends.

"Come on, get on!" yelled one of the warriors as he drew near.

Not waiting for a second, Gameknight jumped behind the rider and drew his two swords. More horsemen came forth, gathering the rest of his companions, then stormed back in the direction they'd came.

By now, the other spiders that had been behind Gameknight and his friends were advancing, clicking their mandibles excitedly. Moving quickly, the warriors charged back toward the opening, but this time it was different. This time, the riders had expert warriors on the back of their steeds, their weapons reaching out with deadly precision to sting the monsters with their razor-sharp blades.

As the horses charged, Gameknight's blades tore into the fuzzy creatures with ruthless accuracy. At the same time, the warrior whose horse he was sharing drew his own iron sword. Together, they carved through the enemies in front as they drove the entire group back, making spider after spider flash red with damage. When they successfully punched through the horde, the riders kept going, heading out onto a brown plain.

"We should go back and finish them off!" Hunter yelled from the back of a powerful white horse. "We can't just leave a group of monsters that size wandering around. They must be destroyed."

"Not yet!" shouted the NPC Gameknight was sitting behind. He guessed he was the squad's commander.

"But we have to fight," Hunter complained. "We can't just run away."

"We aren't running away," the commander replied, then turned and glanced at Hunter with a smile.

Gameknight looked back at the narrow passage. He could see all the remaining spiders flowing out of it like a terrible storm of claws and fangs. The riders galloped out onto the wide, rusty plain, then stopped and turned their horses around to face their adversary. But instead of charging, they kept back, waiting for the spiders to approach.

"What are you doing?" Hunter said as she aimed an arrow at the approaching monsters.

"Wait for it," the commander said in a strong, clear voice.

"But they're getting closer," Hunter complained.

"Hunter, take it easy," Gameknight said. "I have the feeling they know what they're doing."

She gave him a scowl, then lowered her bow and waited.

"Almost there," the commander said, and then he raised his iron sword high over his head. "NOW!" he screamed.

Twenty archers stood up from holes they'd been crouching in and fired out onto the swarm of monsters that were now out in the open. Drawing their arrows as fast as possible, they launched their deadly projectiles into the fuzzy bodies. Not waiting for permission, Hunter leapt to the ground and began firing her own magical arrows, their flaming shafts streaking through the air like bolts of enchanted lightning. In a second, Stitcher was at her side, adding her own shots. Gameknight jumped down and stood guard over the sisters as they fired.

The spiders, realizing the trap, charged straight toward the horsemen, their angry eyes glowing with hatred, hoping to get close enough that their arrows would not be as effective. One of the monsters broke through the chaos and ran toward the two girls. Gameknight leapt forward and attacked the beast. He spun to the left and slashed at the monster, then rolled to the right and attacked its exposed side. Jumping high into the air, he landed on the monster's back, bringing his two swords down in a lethal blow that took the rest of the creature's HP. It disappeared with a pop, dropping Gameknight999 onto the ground on his back. Before he could roll over, a pair of spiders immediately jumped at him. Gameknight brought his diamond sword up in time to block one of the curved claws, but he could see from the corner of his eye that second spider was readying an attack that he wouldn't be able to defend.

The cavalry commander was suddenly there at his side. His iron sword came down on the creature, and it leapt back, away from Gameknight999. Once on his feet, the User-that-is-not-a-user charged into the fray, swinging his dual swords with lethal accuracy. He attacked one spider, jumped to the side to avoid a claw, and swung at another target. With the cavalry commander at his side, he carved through the monster horde, the NPCs fighting next to him just as successfully.

Soon, the archers had whittled down the monsters' HP to the point that the cavalry could charge forward with their swords to finish the creatures. Back in the chasm they had just escaped, Gameknight999 could see three of the spiders limping back into the Bryce. By the amount of damage they had sustained, he guessed they were not likely to survive long.

"Thank you," Gameknight said as he stood next to the nameless, mysterious warrior who'd brought his troops forward to save them all. "How did you—"

"No time for questions. It's getting dark," the warrior said. "We need to get back to our village." He led his horse around by the reins and addressed his troops. "Everyone to the village, fast."

He then leapt up onto his horse and offered the User-that-is-not-a-user a hand. Gameknight put away his swords and jumped up onto the horse. The warrior turned and checked that everyone was ready to ride, then headed across the rolling hills and their village that Gameknight thought must be hidden somewhere beyond.

CHAPTER 13

THE NEXT VICTIM

Gameknight spotted the village just as the sun started to kiss the horizon. They paused for a moment at the top of a tall grass-covered hill, allowing those within the village to clearly see them. It gave Gameknight999 the opportunity to see this new community. It mostly looked like any other grassland village, with wooden houses clustered around a central well and a tall watchtower looming high over the buildings. But there was one fundamental difference about this village: it was fortified to the teeth.

A high wall surrounded all the houses, but instead of being a single block deep, as would be normal for a village, this barricade was four blocks thick, with archer towers located every twenty blocks. Long fortified ramps extended out over the edge of the walls with holes for pouring water or firing arrows on monsters directly beneath. Large gun ports in the walls aligned with the TNT cannons that sat in the village's courtyard, stacks of TNT standing at the ready. When fired, the TNT cannons would launch their projectiles through the holes in the wall, protecting the cannon crew from attack, but letting their deadly cargo reach the attacking forces.

Gameknight also noticed that all across the grassy plain were holes two blocks deep. He was sure these were murder holes, traps into which an unwary monster could fall, allowing a villager to attack their legs from the safety of underground tunnels.

An NPC waved a long red banner from the top of the watchtower, signaling that they'd been seen and it was safe to approach. The horsemen kicked their mounts forward, moving at a trot toward the village. When they reached the fortified walls, a set of outer iron doors swung open, revealing a narrow tunnel. They rode through the narrow passage in single file. At the other end was another set of iron doors that stood closed. Holes in the walls of the tunnel were filled with bristling arrows as archers watched the armed party enter. The far doors opened when the leader gave the correct password, allowing the warriors to finally enter the village, the doors closing quickly behind.

"These are some impressive defenses," Crafter said to the leader.

"We have good cause to be cautious," the leader replied.

"By the way, we thank you for your assistance," Crafter said. "What is your name?"

"I am the village's butcher, but my friends call me Butch," he replied. "Welcome to our village."

Gameknight slid off the back of Butch's horse.

"How is it you happened to be out there in the mesa at the exact moment we needed you?" Digger asked as he approached Gameknight, his pickaxe resting on his shoulder.

"Our scouts saw the fireworks go off in the air and figured it was a signal for help," Butch explained.

"You had scouts out there?" Gameknight asked.

"We have scouts everywhere," Butch replied. "Our village sits near a zombie-town, a skeleton-town, and a creeper hive. Actually, I was surprised when we saw that it was only spiders attacking. You got off easy."

"Easy? There were forty or fifty spiders out there!" Hunter exclaimed.

"We've seen ten times that number at our gates," Butch said. "Forty or fifty are just an annoyance."

"Well, we're certainly grateful that you had that scout out there," Stitcher said.

"We've learned to always be watching," Butch said. "The monster villages around us are always attacking, and we must be ready at all times."

"That is a wise attitude," Crafter said, nodding his head.

Butch turned and looked down at the young boy.

"I've never seen a crafter as young as you," Butch said, an eyebrow raised.

"It's a long story," Crafter replied, casting a knowing grin toward Gameknight. Butch followed the glance, then stepped up to the User-that-is-not-a-user.

"I know who you are, of course. That was nice work with your two swords . . . just like Smithy, right?"

"No one is just like Smithy, I understand," Gameknight said.

Butch nodded in agreement. "Tell me, who are your companions?"

A group of villagers were now beginning to congregate around the newcomers.

"I'm Gameknight999. This is Crafter, Digger, Hunter, Stitcher, and Herder."

Butch and the other warriors bowed their heads to the guests.

A howling sound from outside the fortified village echoed across the grasslands. Gameknight looked at Herder and found the boy was smiling and glancing toward the iron gates. Holding up a hand to signal him to wait, the User-that-is-not-a-user shook his head, causing the smile on Herder's face to dim slightly.

"Wolves, a lot of them," a voice said from the barricade.

Butch looked at Gameknight999, a confused look on his face.

"Those are friends of ours," the User-that-is-not-a-user explained.

"Hmm," Butch said as he considered this idea, then looked at one of the guards.

The warrior pushed a lever on the wall, causing the gates to open. A dozen wolves streaked into the village and headed straight for Herder. The lanky NPC knelt and petted each one, then gave every member of the pack a skeleton bone. Tiny red hearts appeared above each as they devoured the treat.

Gameknight laughed as he saw more confusion filling Butch's eyes.

Crafter stepped forward and spoke in a low voice. "We're thankful that you saved us, and it would be great to stand around and celebrate, but

I need to talk with your crafter. I fear your village is in danger."

"Look around you," Butch said in a loud voice. "I pity the monster army that wants to test their strength against our defenses. We've faced large groups of monsters before. We are not afraid."

"Still, we must talk with your crafter. In private," Crafter insisted.

Just then, a commotion came from the tall stone watchtower. Turning, Gameknight saw an old figure moving through the crowd, his long gray hair hanging in tangled clumps around his shoulders, dark brown eyes staring directly at the newcomers.

"Well now's your chance. Here he comes now," Butch said, pointing to the aged NPC.

Crafter moved forward and held out a hand. The old crafter looked at the young boy before them, then glanced at his black smock with a gray stripe running down the center and smiled. Extending his wrinkled hand, he shook Crafter's hand, then patted him on the back.

"You are far from home, I think," the old crafter said.

"That is indeed true," Crafter replied. "We are here on a quest to stop Herobrine from hurting NPCs across Minecraft."

"Herobrine," the old man croaked. "He's gone. Can you not feel the difference in the fabric of Minecraft? That poisonous creature has been expelled."

"We know that," Gameknight said, getting impatient.

The old crafter looked up at the brash user who had pushed through the crowd, then froze in shock as he saw that no server thread connected him to the server.

"You're the—"

"Yeah, yeah, he's the User-that-is-not-a-user," Hunter said as she moved to Crafter's side. "Get over it. We're here on important business and don't have time for pleasantries."

"Hunterrrr," Stitcher said, rolling her eyes.

"What?" the older sister replied with a harrumph.

"Herobrine has set up traps that are doing a lot of damage to villages across Minecraft," Gameknight999 explained, "and we think this village is his next target."

"Well, I can assure you that's not possible," the old man stopped to cough for a moment. "Because Herobrine is dead, and dead people don't lay traps."

Gameknight could tell this NPC was incredibly old, maybe as old as Crafter had been when they'd first met.

"We were the ones that destroyed Herobrine," he told the crafter. "Well . . . we thought we did. We thought the same thing you think now, that Herobrine is gone forever. But he's been leaving traps and messages for us. Or at least someone pretending to be Herobrine is. It's not as simple as you think."

"Sorry," the crafter replied. "I can assure you, regardless of whether Herobrine is alive or dead, no monsters will breach these walls. They are impregnable. We are quite safe."

The wolves suddenly stopped pacing and all turned to face to the southwest. The pack leader growled as his eyes turned bright red, causing the fur on the other wolves to bristle and stand out as more growls joined their leader.

"What's happening?" Herder asked.

"Nothing, why?" Butch replied.

A banging sound came from atop the watchtower. Looking up, Gameknight could see an NPC striking a piece of armor with the flat of his sword. Once he had everyone's attention, the watcher pointed off to the southwest.

"Quickly, to the walls!" Butcher yelled as he ran for the stairs.

Gameknight sprinted after the warrior, his enchanted diamond sword already in his hand. When they reached the top of the wide, fortified wall, they could see a rider galloping as fast as he could straight toward the village. Behind the rider there seemed to be a series of square shadows forming. In the dim light of dusk, the oranges and reds of the sunset made it difficult to tell what was happening. But one thing was clear to Gameknight: the shadows were closing on the warrior.

Glancing over his shoulder, the rider looked at the square shadows. Kicking his horse into a sprint, he rode faster, straight for the village, but the shadows formed in random places behind him, getting closer and closer. Gameknight and his friends watched from a distance, a feeling of dread building in their stomachs. The rider wasn't going to make it.

They were right. A few moments later, the shadowy blocks finally overtook the horse and rider, and they immediately disappeared.

"What happened?" Butch cried aloud. "Was he teleported or something? What are those shadows?"

Gameknight sighed, for he knew what they were. "Those aren't shadows, they're holes. Herobrine is creating holes in the landscape that probably go all the way down to bedrock, and he's aiming those holes at this village."

"What do we do?" Butch asked, his voice, for the first time, showing a hint of fear.

Gameknight turned and looked at Butch, a look of sadness on his face as he spoke two words:

"We run!"

CHAPTER 14

HOLES

"**E**VERYONE, RUN!" Butcher boomed as he sprinted down the steps.

All around him, villagers ran for the stairs that led down to the ground. Gameknight followed, right behind a group of warriors. He put away his swords and pulled out a shovel, scanning the ground. Suddenly, a hole opened beneath part of the fortified wall far to the left. An entire section of the cobblestone collapsed as a group of NPCs still on top of the wall fell into the void, their cries echoing as they plunged into darkness. Gameknight held back a tear as he listened to the voices. They were not yelling out in fear, for they all knew their fates. Instead, they were saying goodbye to loved ones as they plummeted to their deaths.

Gameknight wanted to run to them, to help somehow, but he knew there was no way to save those who had already vanished into the cavernous holes in the ground. He had to find the sign and kill the redstone that was powering the hidden command block to prevent more NPCs from dying.

"Everyone look for a sign!" Gameknight shouted. "It's got to be here somewhere. Under it there will be—"

The ground right next to him disappeared. He felt a slight breeze when the sandy earth fell away, then a wave of heat burst from the empty shaft. Looking down into the hole, Gameknight saw that the abyss stretched down until it disappeared into the haze, probably descending all the way down to the bedrock. Lava was oozing out of a gap in the square shaft, slowly crawling down the side of the opening, the heat from the lava blasting out as if he were standing next to a furnace.

Wails of grief rose from the villagers as more of their family and friends were consumed by the insidious holes. But none of them stood around and mourned. Instead, they all fled their village and ran for their lives.

We have to find that sign, fast, or this village is doomed, Gameknight thought.

"Gameknight, come on!" a voice said from behind him.

Turning, he found Herder standing behind him.

"We have to get out of this village . . . NOW!"

The lanky boy grabbed Gameknight's armor and pulled him away. They ran around the many gaping holes that now peppered the village, heading for the iron gates. Curving this way and that, Gameknight and Herder made it out of the village, having to leap aside once as the ground crumbled under their feet. They shot through the iron gates that now stood open and out onto the grassy plains that surrounded the village. Many of the NPCs were already there, weeping as they stood and watched their village being slowly and methodically destroyed.

"Don't bunch together!" Gameknight shouted. "If a hole appeared under the group, all of you would be goners. Spread out. We still need to find the signs. Everyone spread out and look for them before your entire village is destroyed!"

The sound of this threat got the villagers moving. They spread out around the landscape, looking for a lone sign, but the grassy plains were large and the sign could be anywhere.

"Gameknight," Herder said.

The User-that-is-not-a-user didn't hear; he was too preoccupied with scanning the darkening landscape, looking for that piece of wood sticking out of the ground that would be this village's salvation.

"Gameknight!" Herder insisted.

"What?" the User-that-is-not-a-user snapped.

"I think I can send the wolves out to find the sign," the young boy said.

"What? . . . um, I mean, do it!"

Herder knelt next to the largest of the wolves and spoke in a calm voice.

"Find the sign."

The wolf instantly sprang into action. He barked a series of commands to the other wolves, then streaked away into the darkness.

Growing impatient, Gameknight paced back and forth, waiting for some signal. He glanced up at the sky. The square face of the sun had dipped completely below the horizon, the stars pushing through the dark veil that stretched overhead. As the sky changed from the crimson glow of sunset to the darkness of night, the moon rose, casting a silvery hue across the grasslands, giving them enough light to see.

The villagers were still running about, looking for the sign, but nervously, being careful not to stray far from each other. They were outside after dark, and they all knew that in Minecraft, night-time was monster time.

A howl pierced the night air off to the left. Not waiting, Gameknight bolted in that direction. As he ran, he could see more sections of the wall disappearing as the holes tore into the landscape where the village stood, each hole exactly like the others, four blocks by four blocks in size. Ahead, he could see the wolves clustered together around a wooden sign, their eyes glowing red in the darkness.

Herder went first and carefully pushed through the pack, clearing a space for Gameknight to enter. With his shovel, the User-that-is-not-a-user dug up the soil around the sign, looking for the cavity that he knew would be there. Almost instantly, his shovel punched through the dirt and found the small chamber. It was lit red from all the redstone torches and powdery traces that were giving off a crimson glow.

"I found it!" Gameknight screamed as he jumped into the hole.

Driving his shovel hard, he slashed at the redstone traces, severing the power from the command block.

The wolves growled as footsteps thundered toward them. Drawing his diamond blade, Gameknight climbed out of the hole and turned to face the threat.

"Put that away you idiot, it's only us," Hunter said as she approached.

"You found the command block!" Crafter said as he ran to his friend's side.

"Yes, I've shut it off," Gameknight said, then turned and faced the approaching NPCs.

The grassy plain was filled with the cries of mourning villagers. Many shouted out the names of their loved ones that had fallen while others remembered friends and neighbors that would never be seen again. Gameknight tried to hold back his own tears of sadness and frustration as he looked upon this shattered community, but he could feel his eyes growing moist. They would never be whole again, and this village would be a permanent reminder of what was lost today.

"Is it safe to go back into the village?" the old crafter said as he neared, two NPCs holding onto the aged leader, helping him to walk.

"Yes," Gameknight replied, "but I don't know why you would want to. There isn't much left."

"This is our home," the old NPC replied. "We must return and rebuild, in memory of those we lost today."

The old man raised a wrinkled hand up into the air, fingers spread wide. The villagers around him did the same, giving a salute to the dead. Gameknight brought his own hand up into the air, angry tears tumbling down his square cheeks. He squeezed his hand into a tight fist as images of all the poor NPCs that had been lost appeared in the back of his mind, their terrified faces likely to haunt him for a long time.

How could Herobrine do this evil thing? Gameknight thought as anger surged through his soul. *If only I'd been quicker at destroying Herobrine, then maybe all these villagers would still be alive.*

Glancing around, he realized he was the only person with his fist still in the air. Slowly, he lowered his arm, his fingers now numb.

"What does the sign say?" Crafter asked.

Gameknight moved around to the front and read the words. "It says, 'ANOTHER VILLAGE GONE BECAUSE OF GK. MORE TO COME. :-) —HB'"

He smashed the sign with his shovel, the splintered pieces flying in all directions.

"This was Herobrine's doing?" the old crafter asked.

Gameknight nodded.

"How is that possible? That monster is dead," Butch said.

Gameknight didn't answer. Uncertainty filled his mind as waves of guilt washed over him.

"It can't be," Gameknight said in a low voice.

"We *think* he's dead. And even if he is, he left these command blocks behind, and must be activating them somehow," Crafter replied. "Either that, or someone's doing his dirty work for him."

The memory of his father smashing the computer that held Herobrine filled his mind, but for some reason, the memory was not as vivid as it had been before. It was as if the memory were changing. *What if he were still alive?* The thought bounced around inside his head as the memory slowly faded into the back of his mind. *No . . . I saw it . . . I know Herobrine is destroyed!* He refused to believe that terrible virus had somehow escaped.

Gameknight turned and stared at the village that was now punctured with holes. A burning rage began to bubble up from within his soul.

"We have to get to the next village before it is destroyed," Gameknight growled, his anger barely held in check. It felt like as soon as one fire was put out, another one immediately flared up. *When would it stop?* he thought. They had to do something other than react to Herobrine's latest trick.

"What direction is the closest village from here?" Stitcher asked.

"There are three villages, all approximately the same distance from us," the old crafter said in a scratchy voice.

"Which one do we go to?" the young girl asked, then turned and looked at Gameknight999.

The User-that-is-not-a-user glanced at Stitcher's questioning eyes, then looked down, afraid to make a wrong decision that would cost more lives.

"Is there one to the northeast?" Crafter asked.

The village's crafter nodded his square head, his gray hair swaying back and forth.

"I think we continue in that direction." Crafter turned to face the butcher. "Send riders to the other villagers and warn them. If something happens, look for the sign and dig. When you find the redstone, break the circuit. Understood?"

Butch looked to a group of warriors and cast them a questioning stare. They nodded, then ran back to the village. In minutes, they were mounting and galloping off in different directions, one group going east, the other south.

"We have to get moving," Digger said, his booming voicing startling some of the villagers. "These command block tricks are starting to happen more frequently. I fear we do not have much time before the next one activates."

"Digger is right," Hunter said. She turned to Butch. "Can we get horses?"

The commander nodded, then glanced at one of the villagers. A young boy ran back to the village with a handful of young NPCs with him. He soon returned with seven horses and a packhorse trailing at the rear.

"Butch, we appreciate the horses, but we only need six," Crafter said.

"I am going with you," the NPC commander said. "Your quest is to find and stop these terrible command blocks. Well, I want to find the person responsible and teach them that they cannot mess with my village and get away with it. I'm coming along, whether you like it or not."

Gameknight nodded at Butch, but the look in the NPC's eyes scared him a little. The villager had such overwhelming hatred and need for revenge that the User-that-is-not-a-user was afraid, not for his friends or even for the monsters they would likely encounter, but for himself.

What if Butch realizes that all of this is my fault? Gameknight thought. *Will he turn his rage on me?*

The image of a furious Butch attacking him made icicles of fear form within the User-that-is-not-a-user's soul.

CHAPTER 15
SHAIVALAK

"**W**hat do you mean, Shorin, when you ssssay that they esssscaped?" Shaivalak asked.

"They had help from the NPCssss at the village," Shorin replied, her voice sounding weak.

Shaivalak looked down on her subject, the bright purple light from her multiple eyes adding to the soft red glow of the nearby redstone torches, painting the gray cobblestone a deep burgundy. Shorin was lying on the ground, completely exhausted. She had been one of the few surviving spiders from the Bryce Canyon battle. The small handful of spiders had nearly consumed their HP trying to get back to the hidden cave and their queen, all to deliver the bad news.

"Gameknight999 and hissss friendssss cannot interfere with the Maker'ssss planssss," the spider queen said, anger filling her bright purple eyes.

"I undersssstand," Shorin said, trying to bow even lower, but her entire body was already pressed onto the cold stone floor.

Shaivalak reached out with a dark claw and brought it to within a hair's breadth of Shorin's head. The spider shook with fear. Shaivalak then moved it gently onto her head and stroked the tiny black hairs back, comforting the sister.

"Bring her mosssss, quickly," the spider queen ordered.

Two of the brothers, cave spiders, scurried forward, each holding a clump of green moss. It was the smaller, blue spiders' job to collect the moss from the cobblestone in dungeons that lay hidden deep underground. They used it to nourish the young spiders just after hatching, but today, it would be used to help Shorin regain her strength.

The sister quickly gobbled up the piles of moss as soon as they touched the ground, her mandibles shoving them into her toothy mouth. After consuming every last morsel, Shorin was finally able to stand on eight wobbly legs and bow her head to Shaivalak.

"Go outsssside, and bassssk in the ssssun atop a nice tall tree ssssomewhere," the spider queen said. "When you are fully healed, return and be ready to fight for the Maker."

"Yessss, my queen," Shorin replied, grateful to still be alive.

As the sister scuttled away, the king of the skeletons stepped forward out of the shadows.

"If one of my skeletons failed me as that one did, I would have killed them," Reaper said.

"That issss why you musssst command from a point of fear," Shaivalak hissed. "My followersssss act out of loyalty and will alwayssss fight harder than your ssssskeletonssss."

She turned and looked at the cave opening far from where they stood. A small flow of lava spilled out of a hole in the wall and oozed down into the darkness. The molten stone cast a warm glow on the entrance and the many skeleton archers that stood near the cave opening, making their bones glow a soft orange. She knew there were more of the pale white monsters hidden in the shadows all throughout the chamber, and yet she still wondered if they would be enough.

"I see you looking at the entrance to the Maker's cave, spider queen, but you need not worry. My skeletons will defend this cavern and the tunnels that lead to it," Reaper said. "Gameknight999 and his army will not be able to penetrate our defenses. I have hundreds of skeletons spread out all through the tunnels up above. We can easily defend it against an army twice our size."

"Reaper ssssoundsssss very ssssure of himsss-self," Shaivalak said.

The skeleton grunted, then thrust his chest out confidently.

"The Maker underessssstimated the Usssser-that-issss-not-a-ussssser many timesss, and the other monssssster kingssss did assss well. Every time, Gameknight999 tricked them ssssomehow. Your overconfidence issss your weaknesssss."

"We shall see," Reaper said, his voice rattling. "Besides, if my skeletons get in trouble, you can simply spawn your spiders into this cavern with that command block next to you."

Shaivalak looked at the orange-checkered block that sat next to her, a lever sitting beside it. A single flip of that switch and the command block would spawn hundreds of spiders in the cave. It was a backup plan, in case the skeletons failed to keep the User-that-is-not-a-user out of the cavern.

"Hopefully, we will not be in need of thissss block," Shaivalak said. "But we musssst expect the unexpected from Gameknight999."

Reaper harrumphed.

"He will fall before my skeletons and beg for mercy. But he will get none. Herobrine defeated him and escaped the Minecraft server, and now we will defeat him as well. When all these command blocks are ready and the timer reaches zero, then Herobrine's revenge will be complete, as his command blocks will destroy all the villages across this server."

The skeleton looked up at the redstone-powered display built into the cavern wall. It showed numbers ticking down from one hundred. Currently, the display showed 48.

"Once the countdown reaches zero, there will be nothing the User-that-is-not-a-user can do," Reaper said.

He let out a hollow, scratchy laugh, his head tilted back until he was looking up at the ceiling. He then brought his gaze back to the nearest command block.

"I see the first test block is set to go off when the timer is at 45," the skeleton king said. "Hopefully, Gameknight999 and his friends will be caught in that village when the command block is triggered. I would love to be there to see him destroyed."

"My ssssisterssss will be there, watching. I will tell you what happenssss, but we musssst ssssstill be prepared. Gameknight999 issss clever and dangeroussss."

"We'll see," Reaper replied, then laughed again, his harsh laugh filling the chamber.

CHAPTER 16

LAVA

They rode through the night, driving the horses as hard as they dared. Around midnight, the party passed from the grasslands biome into the desert, the rolling grass-covered hills transitioning into sandy dunes.

"Gameknight, we must rest," Hunter said.

"No, we can't," he replied.

I can feel Herobrine's next command block getting ready to activate, Gameknight thought.

"We must keep riding so we can reach the next village in time," the User-that-is-not-a-user said.

"Gameknight, we will kill the horses if we continue at this pace," Crafter said. "If that happens, it will take even longer to get to the village than if we had stopped."

He sighed, knowing his friend was right. Pulling on the reins, Gameknight slowed his horse to a walk, the others behind him doing the same. He then glanced about nervously, scanning the desert and looking for threats.

"You need to calm down," Crafter said as he pulled his horse up next to him. "You're so wound up, you're about to explode."

"Don't you see? Herobrine's command blocks have been getting more lethal with each occurrence," Gameknight said in a low voice. "What will it be at the next village? What could be worse than all those holes that almost destroyed every villager, plus us?"

"I don't know," Crafter replied.

"I can't let it happen again," Gameknight mumbled. "I can't let more families be destroyed because of me. The only way I can stop it is if I get there before the command block goes off. It's my responsibility to fix this." He then lowered his voice to a whisper. "This is all my fault. I must do something."

"Gameknight, you can't take the responsibility for—"

A howl pierced the still night air. Gameknight snapped his head in the direction of the sound, then turned and looked at Herder. The lanky boy had a huge smile on his face.

"I sent the wolves ahead to look for the village," Herder said.

Gameknight nodded his approval, then kicked his horse into a gallop.

"Come on!" he yelled as his horse climbed a sand dune.

When he reached the top of the dune, Gameknight could see the desert stretching out before him. Nearby, a flower forest butted up against the sandy terrain, then an extreme hills biome after that. In the distance, he could just make out a massive mountain, bigger than he'd ever seen. It was barely visible through the darkness.

At the bottom of the dune, Gameknight saw a desert village. A huge wall of sandstone and cobblestone surrounded the collection of pale yellow homes. Torches placed on walls and fence posts cast circles of light upon the sandy structures, allowing Gameknight to make out individual features: a blacksmith's house, the animal pens, the village's well, and, of course, the tall sandstone watchtower that rose high up above the community.

Charging down the dune face, Gameknight sprinted for the entrance.

"Open the gates!" Gameknight yelled as he rode. "OPEN THE GATES!"

He could see the villager atop the watchtower turn and face him, then pull out a piece of armor and bang a sword against the iron coat. More torches came to life as the community woke to the alarm. But as he approached the wall, a strange shimmering appeared above the village gates. A block of lava suddenly appeared within the shimmering field. The molten stone slowly flowed downward and spread across the ground, completely blocking the entrance to the village.

Skidding to a stop, Gameknight looked on in horror as more blocks of lava appeared directly over the village. The boiling stone flowed downward, creating glowing orange fingers of that stuck up high in the air. The lava crept downward, flowing across homes and buildings, creating large pools of death across the community. Screams of terrified villagers cut through the silent desert, each one stabbing at Gameknight's soul.

The gates are blocked, and they're trapped in the village . . . what do I do? Gameknight thought.

A flaming arrow streaked past him. Following its path, he saw a block of TNT had been placed next to the protective wall, the flaming shaft of the arrow sticking out. The blinking cube exploded, tearing a huge gash in the wall.

"Now *that's* how you make a door," Hunter said as she dashed by.

Gameknight leapt off his horse, scanning the desert for Crafter. He spotted him approaching off from the right.

"Crafter, give Herder some fireworks!" he yelled to his friend.

The young NPC looked at Gameknight, confused.

"Herder!" the User-that-is-not-a-user shouted in the other direction. "I want you to stay out here and launch a new rocket every minute to show the villagers where to run."

The lanky boy nodded, his long, dark hair falling across his face.

Crafter dropped a handful of striped rockets off with Herder, then followed Gameknight into the village through the hole in the wall. Already, Hunter and Stitcher were directing the NPCs inside toward the opening.

"Everyone, this way!" Gameknight yelled, waving his enchanted sword over his head.

Many of the villagers ran toward them, but even more just stood there, in shock and unable to move. Glancing up into the sky, Gameknight could see more cubes of lava appearing within shimmering fields, hovering in midair over the village, slowly dripping liquid death upon whatever or whoever lay beneath. The wooden roof of a home burst into flames as a stream of lava slowly spread across the structure. Gameknight ran to it and opened the door. He found a young boy and girl inside, afraid to come out.

"It's OK. Come with me," Gameknight said softly as he sheathed his sword. "Your parents are outside. We're going to join them."

The children looked at each other nervously. Glancing up, Gameknight could see flames begin to lick at the blocks of the roof overhead, the orange glow of the lava getting brighter.

Stitcher was suddenly at his side, and approached the children. Holding out her hands, she silently took each of their hands and calmly led them out of the house just as the lava broke through. Once outside of the house, Gameknight picked up the boy while Stitcher lifted the girl. They both ran for the opening. Looking back, he realized they had escaped at the last possible second. The house was now completely engulfed in flame.

The User-that-is-not-a-user stopped one of the villagers and handed them the boy, then ran back into the village. One side of the community was completely blocked off with lava and flames, but he could still hear voices beyond the burning wall of fire. Running to the village well, Gameknight filled a bucket, then charged toward the barrier of fire. He moved up next to the flowing lava and heaved the water forward. The liquid pushed him back a few blocks, but also put out the flames. Where the water touched lava, the molten stone turned to cobblestone and obsidian. Placing a block of dirt on the source of the water, the streaming liquid quickly disappeared. He'd successfully made a small bridge across the flaming barrier. Gameknight jumped over the still-warm stone and charged forward.

"OVER HERE!" Gameknight yelled to everyone trapped on the other side. "COME TOWARD MY VOICE!"

He could hear the sound of running feet, though he could see little through all the smoke. A stream of NPCs suddenly appeared through the haze, some of them wearing singed smocks.

"Come on, this way," Gameknight said as he spun and sprinted for safety.

Many villagers came forth out of the smoke and leapt over the steaming cobblestone, escaping the burning side. But Gameknight could still hear more voices trapped behind flames. More lava spilled down in front of him, creating a wide river of molten stone that was at least a dozen blocks wide. Water could only spread six blocks in Minecraft, and he only had one bucket of water left. This new boiling barrier had completely sealed off the smoky portion of the village, trapping the screaming NPCs behind a wall of flame and lava. The villagers were doomed.

Gameknight could feel a tear trickle down his face as burning rage and overwhelming guilt filled his mind.

"Gameknight, get out of there!" Stitcher yelled from the opening in the wall.

Looking toward the voice, he turned and led the NPCs in front of him to the exit. They raced across their village as it burned to the ground, weaving around new columns of lava as more of the boiling stone appeared overhead. Pools of the deadly liquid began to expand across the ground of the village, making it more and more difficult to get to the opening. Then, just as they were about to start crossing, a lava block formed over the opening in the wall, covering their only way out of the village with liquid death.

What do I do? Gameknight thought. *Where do we go?*

Thankfully, his friends on the other side had prepared for such a setback. Another explosion shook the ground as a new section of the wall disappeared near the animal pens.

"This way!" the User-that-is-not-a-user shouted.

He streaked toward the newly-created escape route, the NPCs following close behind, everyone weaving around expanding pools of deadly lava. When he reached the opening, Gameknight pulled out his pickaxe and shattered the fences of the animal pens while the villagers streamed through the exit. Pigs, chickens, cows, and horses followed the villagers out of the doomed community as more lava appeared overhead.

Gameknight could still hear screaming from within the village, but the area had now become completely covered with lava. There was no escape for those still trapped within.

"Everyone move back away from the wall!" Digger boomed.

Someone grabbed Gameknight's arm and pulled him away from the village. Despite his protests, they led him up to the top of a sand dune where the NPCs had congregated. The village was now completely consumed in flames and lava. Gameknight put his head in his hands, thinking of all the remaining villagers trapped inside, knowing there wasn't any way to help them escape.

"Look!" one of the villagers exclaimed, and Gameknight looked up.

As they all watched, new shimmering fields appeared above the flowing village, even higher up in the air than the lava pouring down. But instead of lava, it was water that fell from on high, flowing over the molten stone that now covered everything. Everywhere the water touched lava, cobblestone or obsidian formed. In seconds, the lava became a sarcophagus of stone, the gray and black cubes creating a large, smoking blister on the surface of Minecraft.

"How could this be?" Gameknight said as he put his face in his hands again.

Tears flowed for what seemed like an eternity. He could still hear the cries of those still trapped with the village, people he'd been too slow to save, but their voices gradually quieted in his mind as the heat and smoke took their final toll. Someone sat down next to him and put their arm around his shoulders. Gameknight looked up to see it was Hunter, her eyes moist as well.

"This wasn't your fault," she said.

"If I'd gotten here sooner, we could have—"

"This was *not* your fault," she said again.

"But all that lava—there were still NPCs trapped in there. I wasn't fast enough to save them." He wiped his eyes on his dirty sleeve. "How could anyone do this to another living creature?"

"I don't know," Hunter replied, her voice cracking with emotion.

The sun began to rise over the eastern horizon, casting the first rays of sunlight on the scene of the disaster. Gameknight stood and hung his head low. He was about to say something when a voice pierced through the gloom.

"Signs over here!" Digger boomed.

Hunter grabbed Gameknight's arm and pulled him to Digger. When he finally looked up, Gameknight saw multiple signs, all lined up in a neat row, one behind the next.

"Gameknight, come read these," Digger said. "I'm sure they were meant for you."

He stepped up to the first. Choking back more tears of guilt, he read.

"It says, 'I'VE BEEN PLANNING THIS FOR A LONG TIME.'" He pulled out his diamond pickaxe and shattered the sign. "The next one says, 'NONE OF THE VILLAGERS SURVIVED, BECAUSE OF GAMEKNIGHT999.'" Gameknight could almost hear Herobrine's mocking voice as he read. He shattered the sign and stepped forward to the next one. "'YOU CAUSED THIS. THEIR DEATHS ARE YOUR FAULT!' Like I didn't know that already," he growled as he destroyed it as well.

Gameknight sighed. He found Hunter at one side, Stitcher at the other. The sisters pressed against him so he could feel their shoulders rubbing against his, their strength ready to help him in any way he needed.

But all I need right now is to just disappear. This is all my fault.

"What does the next one say?" Crafter asked.

Gameknight cleared his throat as he fought back the tears.

"It says, 'NEXT WILL BE ALL THE VILLAGES AT ONCE.'" Gameknight smashed that sign to reveal the last one. "The last one says, 'LAVA FOR EVERYONE! TICK TOCK TICK TOCK . . . :-)'"

The meaning of these last two struck Gameknight hard. He sat on the ground, feeling defeated.

"He's going to do this lava thing on *all* the villages?" the User-that-is-not-a-user moaned. "How am I supposed to stop him?"

Gameknight looked down at the mound of stone and obsidian. Water sources were still spewing liquid that flowed down the sides of the tomb and spread out across the desert. From behind, the User-that-is-not-a-user could hear someone digging with a shovel. They shouted when they found the redstone circuits, then cheered when they broke the redstone lines leading to the command blocks.

Lost in his gloom, he barely took notice. Before him was a monument to his failure. But soon, it would only be the *first* symbol of how the User-that-is-not-a-user had let Minecraft down. When time ran out, all of the villages would be destroyed just like the one below . . . and there was nothing Gameknight could do but watch.

CHAPTER 17
MAP

'*ve let them all down,* Gameknight thought. *All those NPCs that were trapped in the village are now gone.*

The guilt was overwhelming; tears still trickled down his cheeks.

"This is all my fault," Gameknight said, his voice barely audible. He looked down at the ground, defeated.

A hand settled gently on his head. Looking up, Gameknight found Crafter looking down at him.

"Gameknight, we all make choices in our lives," Crafter said, his bright blue eyes boring into his friend as if they looked right into his soul. "And these choices define the kind of person we are and who we want to become. Some people always make the easy decision and take the easy path, while others pick the hard choice that might help other people. You always choose the latter, trying to help as many people as you can. But you cannot help everyone, and you cannot be responsible for everyone."

"But if I had stopped Herobrine sooner, then—"

"If . . . *IF*," Crafter snapped, his calm face now showing a scowl. "You don't know what would have happened if you had done something different. You can't go back in time and do things over. All you can do is live with the choices you've made and try your best to learn from them."

"I know, but—" Gameknight said, but was interrupted again.

"There is no *but* . . . there is only *now*," Crafter said, as if stating some kind of universal truth. "You made your choices and Herobrine made his. Both of you will be held accountable for your actions, just as I am held accountable for my choices as well. Herobrine chose to do this terrible thing. It was his decision and no one else's, and he is the one responsible. You did everything you could to stop him, and finally, you were successful. This is something that we all are proud of. There is no doubt we would have wanted to stop him sooner. We made the best decisions we could, and eventually stopped that monster. But don't think for a second that you are responsible for this village being destroyed because you didn't stop him sooner. That's ridiculous."

Crafter looked down at Gameknight999. Compassion filled his blue eyes.

"Herobrine made the choice to program the command block to dump lava on this community. That monster activated the timers that set all this into motion, and he is responsible for the consequences here. To say you are responsible for this is like saying the rain is responsible for someone getting wet because they didn't take the time to fix their roof." He took a step closer, then knelt in front of his friend. "Our decisions define who we are. Don't let Herobrine choose who you will be."

"That's good and all, but we can't just sit here and do nothing," Hunter said.

"What do you suggest?" Digger asked.

"Well . . ."

"The 'tick tock' must mean he has a timer somewhere," Crafter interrupted.

Gameknight stood, considering Crafter's words, but they hung hollow in his mind. Hunter nudged him in the back, trying to make Gameknight speak, but all he could do was hang his head in shame. Hunter glared at him for a moment, then turned away.

"If we shut off all the timers, then we'll save the villages," Digger said.

"But we have no way of knowing where the command blocks are buried," Hunter said. "We can't go to every village and just wait until the signs appear."

"No, we can't," Crafter said. "But Herobrine probably has a central timer. His sign said he was going to do this to all the villages at the same time. That means he'll have one timer somewhere that will turn on all the command blocks."

"But it's not like we have a map that tells us where his timer is located," Herder said.

Gameknight barely heard any of the conversation. The whole scene was like a dream—no, a nightmare. He felt defeated, the overwhelming sense of guilt hammering at him from all sides.

If only I'd stopped Herobrine sooner. If only I'd been strong enough or fast enough to save these villagers. If only . . . the litany of guilt continued to parade through his mind. But as he spiraled deeper into depression, the light of something Herder said shone through his gloom like a distant beacon.

A map . . .

Gameknight thought about maps. His friends continued to debate what to do next, their words passing through him as if he were a ghost. But that single word seemed to bounce around in his mind . . . *map.*

"But it's not like we have a map that tells us where his timer is located." Herder's words resonated in his mind.

Gameknight remembered something his father had told him. *"You can't focus on your fears, for fear will consume your courage and strength to fight. When you focus on what you can do instead of what you are afraid of, your fear will evaporate and allow you to think."*

The image of his father in his ridiculous monkey face and Superman outfit brought momentary relief from the anger and sadness that was washing over him, and allowed him to think for just an instant. *Focus on what you can do,* he thought. At that moment, Gameknight knew what he could do.

Maybe if they mapped out everything that had happened, he'd see a pattern. As his friends argued around him, trying to come up with a plan, Gameknight stood and pulled a crafting bench out of his inventory, placing it on the ground. Going back into his inventory, he found a compass and a stack of paper. He wasn't sure who'd given him the items and didn't care; right now he was only focused on the immediate task at hand.

Placing the compass at the center of the crafting bench, he quickly placed sheets of paper along the perimeter. Instantly, the items changed into a map, its edges tattered and frayed as if it were ancient.

"What are you doing, Gameknight999?" Crafter asked.

He didn't respond. Holding the map out in front of him, Gameknight could see the stone-covered village at the center, the desert wrapping around it on all sides.

"It's too small," Gameknight muttered.

"What did you say?" Digger asked.

He ignored them and concentrated on his task.

Putting the map back on the crafting bench, Gameknight placed pieces of paper around the edges. The map suddenly grew bigger, the image zooming out. Inspecting it, he could see the area the chart covered was now larger, but it was still too small. He repeated the process two more times, until he had a full-sized map.

"What are you doing?" Hunter asked. "Planning a trip or something?"

"Hunterrrr," Stitcher chided.

The older sister rolled her eyes.

The User-that-is-not-a-user suddenly looked up from the map. He was shocked to find everyone staring at him, questions on all their square faces.

"Ahh . . . I was just thinking about something Herder said about a map," Gameknight explained as he used his sleeve to dry the tears from his cheek.

He pulled out an item frame and placed it on the side of a nearby block of sandstone. He then placed the map in the frame. Stepping back, he stared at it for a minute, then another minute, then another. He stood like a statue, staring at the map, examining every aspect . . . then a revelation burst within his mind.

"He's pointing us straight to it," Gameknight whispered.

The NPCs had long turned away from Gameknight, believing that they had better things to do than stand around and watch him tinker. They'd begun arguing again about what to do next, many of them weeping aloud for those lost under the lava. Only Crafter still stood next to him, listening.

"What?" Crafter asked. "Tell us what you see here."

"If you look," Gameknight explained, "you can see where Herobrine's first command block attacks occurred, at the bottom left of the map, in your village." He pointed to the spot with a stubby finger. Anger began to bubble up through the haze of guilt. Some of the villagers muttered angry curses. "And then the rain of bones and snowballs . . . a little farther up and to the right." Gameknight could hear Crafter hiss, his anger reaching the level of Gameknight's. "The location of the falling sheep was up and to the right as well, and then the attack by the wolves right here." The User-that-is-not-a-user looked up from the map and glanced at Herder. He could see the lanky boy's eyes burn with anger, as did his own, as they all relived Herobrine's terrible tricks. His sense of guilt was quickly becoming a fading memory, as rage pushed everything aside. Gameknight999 looked back down at the map. "So you can see, all of Herobrine's attacks were lying along a line that pointed right to this village, and to . . ."

The User-that-is-not-a-user realized his voice had grown louder and louder as his anger blossomed, and those around him had become very quiet. Looking away from the map, Gameknight found all eyes focused on him.

"I think I know how to find Herobrine's timer," the User-that-is-not-a-user said. "All of Herobrine's attacks have been along a line that goes from Crafter's village to this village. He did these attacks so that it would lead us here. That vile creature wanted us to witness this attack and feel powerless to do anything about it!" Suddenly, Gameknight realized he was shouting.

"That sounds like Herobrine," Crafter agreed.

Gameknight took a deep breath and brought his anger under control.

"But in his arrogance, he actually showed us where his timer was hidden," Gameknight said, the anger beginning to boil. He moved his finger along the map, starting at Crafter's village, moving it along the trajectory of their adventure until it landed at the current village. He then moved his finger along that path until it came to a gigantic mountain that filled the top corner of the map.

"What is that mountain?" Gameknight asked, jabbing at the map with his finger.

Crafter looked at the map, then turned and pointed to the huge mountain that was just visible on the horizon.

"You mean that?" Crafter asked.

Gameknight nodded his head.

"That's Olympus Mons, the largest mountain in Minecraft," Crafter said.

Gameknight stared off into the distance. He knew it was part of an extreme hills biome, and that there would be countless tunnels and caves under that mighty peak. That was where they would find Herobrine's timer.

"All of Herobrine's attacks point right to that gigantic mountain," the User-that-is-not-a-user said. "And that flagrant symbol of his ego is just the kind of place he'd choose to hide such an evil mechanism."

He turned from the mountain and looked at all the survivors around him, then glanced at the destroyed village behind them. Tears streamed down numerous faces as feelings of grief still ravaged many of the NPCs. Gameknight felt tears welling up in his own eyes again, and for the first time, did not try to hold them back.

"I'm sorry I couldn't save your village," he said, his voice cracking with emotion. "I was too late in stopping Herobrine, and I allowed him to set up these terrible command block attacks. It's my fault all this destruction happened, and I wouldn't blame any of you for hating me."

Gameknight waited for some reply, but only received silence.

He sighed.

"If I just stay here and feel sorry for myself, then I know what will happen. If I do nothing, then I guarantee the outcome. If I just give up and hide, I know all of the villages will meet the same fate as your own."

He felt someone move next to him. Turning, he found Hunter at his side, her enchanted bow in her hand. She gave him a nod, then turned and glared at the rest of the villagers.

"Herobrine led us here, to this village, so that we would witness what happened and cower in despair. Well, I'm not gonna do that." Gameknight's voice became louder. "He probably has hundreds of monsters in the tunnels under that mountain, but

I don't care. I bet that's where his timer is located, in a cave somewhere. I'm going there to destroy it. I'm tired of waiting for something to happen, and then reacting and trying to limit the damage. We're just dancing to Herobrine's tune, and I'm tired of that. No more villages will suffer the terror that occurred here today."

Stitcher and Herder moved to his other side, the pack of wolves crowding around him.

"I can't do it alone," the User-that-is-not-a-user said, "nor with just a handful of people." He paused for a moment and looked at the NPCs, staring into as many tear-soaked eyes as he could find. "You've all lost so much, and it's not fair for me to ask you for more . . . so I'm asking for all of the villages still in danger. Who among you will help me to stop this disaster from happening all over Minecraft?"

Looking at the faces that surrounded him, Gameknight saw the tears had stopped flowing. The red eyes that had once been filled with grief were now filled with anger. One of the wolves growled softly for a moment as it stared up at Olympus Mons. The desert became eerily quiet. The gentle breeze that flowed from east to west caused the few dried shrubs nearby to move, creating a gentle rustling sound that seemed like thunder in Gameknight's ears.

And then a strong voice sounded across the sandy landscape.

"I will accompany you," Butch said as he stepped forward. The big NPC cast his gaze across the surviving NPCs, then turned back to Gameknight999.

All of the other villagers took a step closer, their strength crowding around the User-that-is-not-a-user.

"All of us will accompany you," Butch added, his voice echoing across the empty desert. "We will stop Herobrine's revenge and laugh in the faces of his minions."

The NPCs cheered, the anger at the destruction of their village carved deep in angry scowls across their brows. They patted Gameknight on the back as spare weapons and armor were distributed. Butch took charge, sending villagers out to collect horses and livestock that were ambling about near the smoking cobblestone tomb. He organized them into squads, then assigned some NPCs to cavalry and others to the ranks of archers. In minutes, the confused group of villagers had been transformed into an army, ready for vengeance.

"Nice speech," Crafter said as he moved behind the User-that-is-not-a-user. "But you're still wrong about it being your fault."

"That doesn't really matter right now, does it?" Gameknight said.

"No, it doesn't," his friend replied as he collected the map and crafting bench.

Turning to the mountain, Gameknight stared up at the massive pile of stone and granite. He could feel Herobrine's malicious touch under that mountain, and knew that the fate of Minecraft would soon be decided in its dark tunnels and caves. Looking around, the weight of responsibility for all these lives around him, and for all villagers everywhere, was like a leaden cloak slowly crushing him.

But he refused to yield. Gameknight refused to play this deadly game on Herobrine's terms. That terrible virus left his mark on Minecraft, and now, today, it was time for the User-that-is-not-a-user to erase that mark . . . forever.

CHAPTER 18
TO OLYMPUS MONS

They moved by day and hid at night as the army of NPCs moved across the landscape toward the massive mountain. Every horse held two riders, and still, people had to walk. Slowing his horse, Gameknight leapt off and handed the reins to a carver that had been on his feet for a while, giving the NPC a bit of a rest. Many of the mounted warriors were doing the same, rotating between walking and riding. They all knew that everyone needed to be rested when it came time to fight.

"I wonder how this mountain got its name," Crafter said as it loomed in front of them.

Gameknight looked to his right and found his young friend walking next to him, having handed his horse off to a cobbler and a baker.

"I don't know," Gameknight answered. "But the strange thing is, I know that name, Olympus Mons. I remember from my science teacher, Ms. Northrop. She was all into the planets, especially Mars."

"Mars? Planets?" Crafter asked.

"I'll explain later," Gameknight said. "But the thing is, Olympus Mons is a mountain on the planet Mars. I remember her saying it was three to four times higher than the highest mountain on earth, something like fifteen miles high."

"Miles? Earth?"

"Yeah . . . some other things I'll add to the list," he replied. "But anyway, it's the tallest thing anywhere known to people in the physical world."

"So it seems to be named appropriately," Crafter said.

"True, but how did a thing in Minecraft get named after a thing in the physical world?" Gameknight asked.

Crafter shrugged.

They walked in silence until they came to the end of the biome, a flowered forest awaiting them. Everyone breathed a sigh of relief when they left the heat of the desert and moved into the temperate climate of the forest. A cool breeze blew from east to west, carrying with it the fragrant smell of flowers. The mixture of sweet aromas enveloped the party as they brushed past yellow dandelions, deep red poppies, sky-blue orchids, and tall lavender lilacs, all standing out against the lush green grass of the forest floor. Every color one could imagine was represented in these flowery fields. As they climbed a small hill and looked down upon the forest floor, the colors reminded Gameknight of a million rainbow sprinkles atop scoops of emerald green ice cream. It was fantastic.

But it wasn't long before something felt wrong.

Drawing his diamond sword, Gameknight glanced around, surveying the landscape. All he could see were flowers and grass and trees, and, of course, the towering form of Olympus Mons, growing larger with every step.

"Gameknight, what's wrong?" Crafter asked.

The User-that-is-not-a-user swiveled his head from left to right, then turned around and walked backward, checking behind the army.

"Ahh . . . what?"

"I said, what's wrong?" Crafter asked again.

"I don't know," he answered. "Something just doesn't feel right."

"Maybe all these flowers have made you nervous?" Stitcher said with a smile. "They do look pretty terrifying."

"No, that's not it," Gameknight replied, not really listening. "Herder . . . where's Herder?"

"Here," replied a squeaky voice off to the right.

"Herder, send your wolves out," Gameknight ordered as he drew closer. "Have them patrol our perimeter."

"But I don't see anything nearby," the boy complained.

"Exactly. There are no animals nearby, only us," Gameknight replied. "Send them out."

The lanky boy nodded, then knelt next to the pack leader. He whispered something Gameknight could not hear, then stood and gave him a wide smile. The largest wolf, the alpha male, gave a strange series of barks, then silently ran off into the forest, each of the other wolves in the pack heading off in a different direction. In seconds, the furry white animals disappeared amid the multicolored landscape.

Gameknight gave a sigh of relief, but still felt uneasy. Out of the corner of his eye, he saw something sparkling with an iridescent purple glow.

Turning, he found Hunter had her bow out, an arrow notched. She, too, was scanning the forest, her eyes narrowed and a scowl carved into her square face. Gameknight moved to her side.

"You feel it too?" the User-that-is-not-a-user asked.

She nodded, her bright red curls bouncing like crimson springs.

"What do you think it is?" he asked.

"I don't know . . . but I don't like it," she replied.

"Yeah, I'm with you," Gameknight replied. Scanning the group, he found Digger and ran to his side. "Digger, something's going on."

"What is it?" the big NPC replied, pulling his huge pickaxe out from his inventory.

"I don't know," he replied, "but we need to be ready. Send out the scouts. Everyone else runs."

"Got it," Digger replied, then started shouting out orders.

"What's going on?" a voice asked from behind.

Gameknight turned and found Butch behind him, his shiny iron chestplate reflecting the colors of the flowers, making him appear to be wearing some kind of magical rainbow armor.

"I don't know what it is, but something just feels wrong," he said as he started to pick up his pace. "You should go watch the left side of our formation."

The NPC nodded and veered off to the left.

"Crafter, you watch the right side!" Gameknight shouted. "Hunter, Stitcher: I want you two up front. I'll watch the rear."

He slowed to allow the army to move past him. He scanned the landscape, looking for anything strange. Glancing upward, he could see the sun was beginning to approach the horizon. They didn't have long until sunset arrived, and he wanted to be someplace defensible when that happened.

Ahead, Gameknight could see Olympus Mons was getting even closer. The end of the flower forest biome was now visible. The gray hue of the extreme hills biome that came next looked pale compared to the colorful forest, the endless gray making his eyes beg for color. They would likely make it to the foot of the mountain by nightfall; maybe there would be a place to camp there.

And then he heard it: the breaking of a branch high up in the forest canopy. Glancing up at the trees, he scanned the branches and leaves for monsters. But the oak trees were thick, with branches that overlapped enough to completely block out the leafy rooftop. Gameknight searched the ground for anyone that might have stepped on a stick or fallen branch, but the forest floor was clear of debris. The sound had definitely come from up there.

I don't like this, Gameknight thought. *Not at all.*

A howl echoed through the forest from behind.

"Monsters!" Gameknight yelled. "Everyone run for the mountain!"

The wolf howled again, then growled and barked as if it were in a battle for its life. The furry creature yelped once, then fell silent.

This isn't good.

As he ran, a clicking sound came from the treetops. At first, it sounded as if it were just a single spider, but he knew they would never be that lucky.

"Faster . . . run faster!" the User-that-is-not-a-user yelled.

The clicking sounds from the trees increased as more spiders joined the percussive symphony.

The NPCs ran as fast as their legs could carry them, each of them knowing this was a race for their lives. Mounted horsemen peeled away from the main army and moved back with Gameknight999, ready to slow the army that stalked them overhead. Hunter rode up to him with a riderless horse. Holding the reins out, she gave the horse to her friend. In a smooth, practiced motion, Gameknight leapt up into the saddle and urged the animal forward.

"Hunter, get your bow out," Gameknight yelled.

"What am I shooting at?" she asked.

"You'll know," he replied with a smile.

Moving forward, Gameknight darted back and forth through the forest. As he neared a tree, he put a block of wood against the trunk, then a cube of TNT above it. The other warriors saw what he was doing and helped out, placing the blocks of wood so that Gameknight could focus solely on the explosives.

"Wait until the clicking gets near," Gameknight said, but his voice was lost in the sound of an explosion.

Fire erupted behind them as the first block of TNT detonated. The top of the tree simply disappeared in an enormous fireball, allowing the clear blue sky to shine through.

The clicking sounds became more agitated, but Gameknight tried to ignore the sound of the approaching spiders. He need to focus all his attention on getting as many blocks of TNT in place as he could while the army ran for Olympus Mons.

A flaming arrow streaked through the air and found another red-and-white striped cube. Another blast of flame enveloped the treetop, tearing a gaping wound in the leafy canopy. Through the smoke,

Gameknight could see blazing red eyes peering at him . . . lots of them.

Now the clicking sounded like a cricket storm as more spiders joined in on the pursuit. Some of the spiders fell through the openings in the treetops and ran after the fleeing NPCs. Mounted warriors rode out to meet those spiders, quickly dispatching them before their numbers could increase.

Another arrow shot through the air, finding its target. Gameknight glanced at Hunter as the TNT exploded. She flashed him a satisfied grin, then notched and fired another arrow.

More spiders were falling through to the ground. Their numbers were increasing quickly, making it hard for the small group of cavalry to deal with them. Gameknight glanced back and saw one NPC fall from his saddle as a spider's claw hit his leg. The warrior landed hard, flashing red, but other cavalry rode to his aid, pushing back the attacking monsters so that the wounded villager could get back on his horse.

"Cavalry, stay close to the rest of the army!" Gameknight yelled. "We can't separate our forces."

He knew getting broken up into small groups in battle was risky. A wise commander could pick you off more easily that way, one at a time, making it possible for a smaller army to defeat a larger force. History was replete with examples of this, and Gameknight had heard many of the stories from his social studies teacher.

"Everyone, hurry!" Gameknight yelled. "Head for the mountain."

Ahead, he could see the end of the forest and the beginning of the extreme hills biome. Looming high over them was the massive mountain, the sides steep but climbable. Unfortunately, that meant that the spiders could follow as well, but Gameknight knew they would have an easier time fighting an enemy they could see, rather than one that could hide in the trees and drop behind their lines.

The NPCs quickly climbed up the face of Olympus Mons, leaving the forest behind. Gameknight sped ahead of the main force, climbing the slope faster than those on foot. When he was high enough, he turned and looked back at the forest.

He gasped. There were at least a hundred spiders across the treetops, their dark, fuzzy bodies blotting out the green leaves, giving the trees a diseased look. As if on cue, the monsters all turned their multiple red eyes toward Gameknight999. The fury in their stares was terrifying.

How are we going to fight that many spiders? Gameknight thought.

"Everyone, run as fast as you can!" the User-that-is-not-a-user yelled.

Seeing their prey begin to escape, the spiders descended from the treetops, lowering themselves on long strands of silk. It looked to Gameknight like some kind of deadly black rain as they emerged through the leaves.

Kicking his horse into a sprint, he shot down the mountain's face and skidded to a stop at the rear of their army. He turned the horse toward the approaching mob, drawing his iron sword with his left hand and his diamond blade with his right. His mount gave off a nervous whinny as the monsters clicked with evil excitement.

Then, out of nowhere, a dozen wolves moved to his side, their growls drowning out the sound of the clicking monsters. This drew eight hundred eyes to Gameknight999, all of them blazing with hatred.

"I don't know how I'm going to stop this many," Gameknight muttered to himself, "but I refuse to let Herobrine and his monsters have their way." He then raised his voice so that it rang across the stony mountain, filled with confidence. "You aren't getting past me, spiders. FOR MINECRAFT!"

The warrior and wolves all charged forward.

CHAPTER 19

SPIDERS

The spiders stopped their advance at the sight of the single warrior and enraged wolves charging toward them. Gameknight could hear many of them clicking their sharp mandibles together in anticipation of the one-sided massacre that was about to happen.

"FIRE!" came a voice from behind him.

Gameknight recognized it as Hunter's voice. On cue, arrows streaked down from the mountainside, tearing into the spider ranks and making the fuzzy monsters flash red as they took damage.

"Get up here, you idiot!" Hunter yelled.

Skidding to a stop, the User-that-is-not-a-user glanced over his shoulder. He could see the army's archers lined up behind blocks of cobblestone, all of them firing down upon the spiders. Gameknight pulled his horse around and raced for the line of defenders.

"Wolves, follow!" he shouted.

The furry creatures immediately pivoted and moved up the mountainside right behind the

User-that-is-not-a-user. When he reached the defensive line, he dismounted and gave his horse to one of the younger NPCs, who was already holding the reins of a dozen other mounts. Drawing his enchanted bow, he added his own arrows to the storm.

The spiders charged up the mountainside despite the deadly rain coming down upon them. They tried to zigzag to avoid the arrows, but there were so many of them it was hard for the archers to miss. But even with all the damage the archers were doing, there were too many monsters approaching, and if they stood their ground, Gameknight knew they were doomed.

"We need to fall back," he said to Crafter, who had appeared at his side during the battle.

"Agreed."

"Have the old and the young move up higher on the mountain," Gameknight explained. "Then take half the archers and form a new defensive line." He looked up the mountainside. "I see something that looks like a hollow or cutout on the side of the mountain. Head for that."

"But how are you going to keep the spiders back?" Crafter asked. "If we take half the archers with us, you'll be overrun."

"I have an idea that will buy us some time," Gameknight said with a smile.

Crafter nodded, then turned and started giving orders, moving people and horses up the slope. Digger moved forward and took half the archers up the hill while the remaining ones kept firing.

Gameknight moved between two villagers and started firing his enchanted bow. Flaming arrows streaked down toward the spiders, igniting the fuzzy creatures. He could see additional flaming arrows coming from the left and right side of the defensive line; Gameknight knew these would be coming from Hunter and Stitcher. But even with all their arrows, the spiders were getting closer and closer.

Some of the NPCs were stepping back, moving away from their cobblestone blocks. Gameknight could see they were getting scared as the black wave of claws and fangs drew closer.

"Stand your ground!" Gameknight yelled, his voice filled with confidence. "We have to give those above us time to get set. We cannot retreat. This is the day when we say NO MORE to Herobrine's monsters!"

The villagers heard the confidence and defiance in his voice and took a step forward. They fired their bows even faster, trying to chip away at the wall of spiders that was moving up the mountainside.

"Gameknight, they're getting closer!" Hunter yelled from the far end of the defenses. "We need to do something soon."

"Don't worry, I have an idea."

"Am I going to like it?" she asked.

"Absolutely," he replied.

Leaning to the left, Gameknight whispered his plan to the NPC beside him.

"Pass it on," he said to the villager, and then turned and told the villager on his other side the same thing.

In minutes, the remaining defenders knew what to do and were waiting for the signal. The spiders were now within four blocks of their defensive line. Gameknight could almost count the hairs around their furious, hateful eyes.

"Gameknight, if they get any closer, I'll be wearing this spider as a hat!" Hunter yelled.

"OK, everyone ready?" the User-that-is-not-a-user yelled. The villagers grunted their affirmation. "NOW!"

As one, the warriors all pulled out buckets of water and dumped them before the spidery mob. The water flowed down the mountainside and carried the monsters back down the hill as it rushed down, setting them back a dozen blocks, if not more.

"Everyone up the hill!" Gameknight yelled.

The NPCs turned and ran. When they reached the cutout, the archers started firing again. This time, it was all of them, thirty archers firing down on all the advancing monsters.

Turning from the battle, Gameknight looked at the hollow they were standing in. It looked like a massive hole had been carved out of the mountain from above. The ground was rough and uneven, most of it covered with grass. Clearly, this was not something cleared out by pickaxes; it was something else. Far overhead, there were long rows of cobblestone that stretched straight out from the mountainside and extended high over the recession. It looked as if the cutout was even with the end of these overhead stone structures. It reminded him of when Gameknight and his sisters had dropped dog treats down on their dog, Barky the Physics Dog, from the branches of a tall tree in their backyard. The ones that Barky missed shattered on the ground, creating a circle of doggie-treat dust beneath the tree limb that was eventually licked up.

Maybe we could do something similar here, he thought.

Pulling out blocks of cobblestone, Gameknight moved to the edge of the alcove and started placing blocks on the ground in a line that extended out into the open air. Carefully standing on the edge of the rocky line, he placed block after block until the single-block path extended far out from the mountainside. From the end, Gameknight could look down and see the spiders directly below him.

"Gameknight, what are you doing?" Digger asked.

"I'll explain later," he replied. "Just build what I've built. Get a bunch of villagers to do it, too."

Putting away his pickaxe, Digger motioned to a group of villagers, then pulled out a stack of cobblestone and began mimicking his friend. In no time, they had a dozen long rows of stone sticking out from the side of Olympus Mons.

The spiders looked up at Gameknight and Digger as they advanced up the hill, ignoring the rain of arrows that was falling upon them.

"Anyone with TNT, get on the end of the cobblestone," Gameknight said.

The NPCs put away their bows and moved carefully out onto the stony lines.

"Now, place blocks of TNT on the side and light them," the User-that-is-not-a-user directed.

Leaning over, Gameknight put a block of TNT on the side of the cobblestone, then lit it with a redstone torch. The cube started blinking, and as it did, it fell down from the ledge, landing among the spiders. It exploded, tearing into the monster horde with a flaming vengeance. As he watched, more blinking cubes fell onto the monsters and detonated. The spiders were thrown in all directions, their bodies flashing red.

"Keep placing the TNT!" Gameknight yelled.

They put the red-and-white striped blocks down as fast as they could, dropping countless bombs on the terrifying monsters. The explosives devastated the mob, tearing HP from the fuzzy bodies without remorse. The spiders tried to push forward, but with every advance, the blocks of TNT smashed the spiders with a relentless fist.

As the explosives fell, they carved a deep hole in the mountainside. Gradually, it began to fill with XP and spider silk as the TNT smashed the attacking spider army to shreds. In minutes, only a handful of the monsters remained.

"Warriors, draw swords and attack!" Crafter yelled.

The wolves howled with angry excitement as they shot down the mountainside ahead of the warriors.

"Leave one alive," Gameknight said as he leapt off the cobblestone.

With his two swords drawn, he bolted down the hill and crashed into the spiders, slashing to the left, then swinging to the right. He was sure the spiders knew they were defeated, but they made no attempt to flee. They continued the fight, even though now they were the ones outnumbered.

Finally, only one spider remained. The lone monster had backed into the newly-formed recession in the side of Olympus Mons. It was exhausted, and the NPCs could tell its HP was nearly depleted.

Gameknight put away his iron sword and pulled out his shield. With his diamond sword in his right hand, he approached the monster. The spider looked up at the User-that-is-not-a-user with complete hatred in its multiple eyes.

"You cannot sssstop ussss," the spider hissed. "Shaivalak will be ready for you."

"Tell us where your queen is and we will spare your life," Gameknight said.

The spider laughed, then clicked her mandibles together.

"You are no match for Shaivalak," the spider said, her eyes beginning to dim. "The queen issss ready to call more ssspidersssss at the flick of a ssssswitch. You will not ssssstop what hassss already begun."

Gameknight took another step closer and began to speak, but the monster leapt straight at him, her wicked curved claws extended. He raised his shield, letting the spider smash against the protective rectangle, then hit her with his sword. She disappeared with a pop, leaving behind more XP and silk.

"What do you think she meant by that?" Gameknight asked Crafter, who stood behind him.

"A flick of a switch? Maybe it's a command block thing?" Crafter said.

Gameknight nodded.

"We have to find Shaivalak and stop Herobrine's timer as quickly as we can," Gameknight said.

"But where do we start looking?" Stitcher said. "The tunnel that leads to his timer could be anywhere."

"I think you all need to come up here," a voice said from above.

Gameknight looked up and saw Herder leaning over the edge of the cutout, his long black hair hanging down over his face. They ran up the hill to find he had retreated all the way to the back of the cutout. In the shadows, Gameknight hadn't noticed the sign placed on a stone block. Right next to it was a hidden tunnel entrance that curved its way behind a wall of rock and into the bowels of the

Mons. Without the sign, which was hard enough to see, they never would have noticed the tunnel.

"What does the sign say?" Gameknight asked.

"It's too dark, I can't see it," Herder said.

Digger pulled out a torch and placed it against the rock wall. Gameknight leaned forward. He could tell by the cracks in the sign that it was ancient; it had clearly been here for a long, long time. As he read the words, the User-that-is-not-a-user was confused.

"It says 'GK was here.' But how is that possible?" Gameknight said.

"Have you been here before?" Crafter asked.

The User-that-is-not-a-user shook his head.

"I've never seen Olympus Mons before, much less this sign and hidden tunnel," he explained. "This is all new to me."

"Well, I think this is a good a place to start our search as any," Hunter said. "And it already has the GK sign of approval." She smiled.

"OK," Gameknight replied. "Then let's go."

Reaching up to adjust his armor, the User-that-is-not-a-user pulled out a torch and stepped into the passage. As he moved through the narrow tunnel, Gameknight imagined all the villages that were counting on him to find Herobrine's timer and stop it from destroying everything. The thought of all those lives depending on him made him shudder with fear.

If only I'd stopped him sooner, Gameknight thought as he plunged into the darkness.

CHAPTER 20

INTO THE DARKNESS

G ameknight moved through the narrow opening in the rock, glancing up at the ancient sign as he entered the passage, confused. The tunnel was only one block wide and two blocks high. It extended four blocks straight into the mountain before it turned to the left, then to the right, then left again, zigzagging deep into the rock. With the multiple turns, the light from outside was easily blocked, making the torch in Gameknight's hand the only source of illumination.

After more turns, the tunnel finally led them to a large room that looked to be some kind of gathering chamber. It was roughly square with a flat stone floor and walls that were poorly shaped. It was wide, at least twelve blocks across and another twelve blocks deep, but its height was shocking. The ceiling must have been at least twenty blocks high and was barely visible in the torchlight. At the far end of the room was a single redstone torch. It lit an opening that was likely a continuation of the passage. The crimson light showed quartz blocks that had been placed over the opening in a large arc. They had been placed every so often along the arc, creating the likeness of a huge mouth, the quartz blocks forming monstrous teeth. The tunnel on the far side looked as if it were leading down the fictitious creature's throat.

"This must be Herobrine's work," Crafter said. "No other person in Minecraft would try to make a tunnel appear so purposely terrifying."

Gameknight nodded his head. Turning, he looked at all the villagers that stood in the tunnel behind him, the torches held by many of the NPCs casting circles of light across their uncertain boxy faces. There were probably fifty villagers with them. Some were armored, but not enough; some held swords, but many only had shovels and hoes. Fortunately, all had bows, which had been decisive in the last battle. But in the narrow confines of these tunnels, Gameknight thought grimly, archers would be relatively ineffective.

How can this ragtag army defeat Herobrine's monsters and at the same time stop whatever trap he has planned for Minecraft? Gameknight thought.

"Well?" Hunter asked.

Gameknight looked at her, confused.

"Are we gonna go in and say hello?" she continued. "Or are we just staying out here and admiring the scenery?" Hunter gave Gameknight a mischievous grin.

"Yeah, we're going in," the User-that-is-not-a-user replied with a sigh.

"Finally," Hunter replied and took a step forward.

Gameknight suddenly realized that something was wrong. Reaching out, he grabbed the back of her armor and jerked her back.

"What's the deal?!" she exclaimed.

"Wait," Gameknight replied. "This is too easy . . . I don't trust it."

"Would some monsters make you happier?" Hunter asked.

Gameknight ignored her questions and looked at the room. There was something here he didn't like. He could feel it, but couldn't see it, not yet. Pulling out a block of stone, he turned and faced Crafter.

"Do you have a rope with you?" he asked.

"Of course, I always have one," Crafter replied. "My great-uncle Farmer once said . . ."

"Crafter, not now. Just give me the line."

"Oh. Sorry, here you go."

Gameknight took the rope and tied it to a block of stone.

"Everyone stand back," Gameknight said as he started to swing the block around in a circle.

Spinning it faster and faster, he launched the block into the cave entrance, the rope stretching out into the passageway ahead. The stone landed with a thud on the sandy floor.

"That *was* exciting," Hunter said sarcastically. Stitcher punched her in the arm.

"Hunter, be nice," the younger sister chided. The older just smiled.

Gameknight ignored the two girls and focused on the block of stone. Slowly, he pulled on the line and dragged the stone toward the entrance. It scraped and tumbled across the ground, the sounds echoing off the passage walls.

"This is interesting," Hunter said, "but . . ."

Before she could finish the sentence, an explosion shook the walls as blocks of TNT detonated around the tunnel opening, tearing a massive hole in the ground. Sand and rock flew through the air as a ball of fire blossomed to life and lit the chamber with a momentary flash of light. Gameknight fell backward as the force of the blast shoved him in the chest, falling into the stout form of Butch, who stood right behind. Fortunately, no one was hurt; the explosion had been deep within the chamber. It had been a trap, probably been meant to kill any intruders—like them.

A hand reached down to Gameknight. Reaching up, he took it and stood, facing Butch, Crafter at his side.

"Apparently we were expected," Butch said through gritted teeth.

Crafter nodded as he looked from the butcher to Gameknight999.

"How are we going to get through these tunnels if they're rigged with traps?" Gameknight asked.

"Don't worry," Butch said. "A trapper came with us from the last village. They can lead us through."

"What?" Gameknight asked, but his question was stopped by Butch's upheld hand.

"Trapper, come forward," Butch yelled. "We need your skills up here."

They could hear confused voices from the back of the army as one of the NPCs moved forward.

"What's a trapper?" Gameknight asked. "I've never heard of them."

"A trapper is a person that sets traps to catch game," Butch explained. "They don't necessarily use arrows or swords, but tricks and snares to catch animals for the village. They have the keenest eyesight so that they can find the best place to put a snare, and have the most nimble of fingers so that they can build their traps. Trappers are rare, but very useful."

"I'm looking forward to meeting him," Gameknight said.

Butch laughed.

The NPC pushed through the crowd and finally came to the front. Gameknight was surprised to find that it was a girl about Hunter's age, with long blonde hair flowing down her back and shoulders. Her bright blue eyes bore right into Gameknight; they rivaled Crafter's in shocking beauty and intensity. Her smock was a grass green with a brown stripe the color of tree bark running down the center. Butch gave Gameknight a wry smile as he introduced the newcomer to him.

"Gameknight999, this is Trapper," Butch said. "*She* is famous among the villages in this section of Minecraft for being the best trapper around. If anyone can see the traps that lie waiting for us, it's her."

Trapper's square cheeks turned red as she blushed over the introduction.

"Thank you, Butcher, but I'm just a trapper like all the rest. I'm nothing special," she said.

"We'll be the judge of that," Butch replied. "Please, lead the way."

He held his hand out, gesturing to the tunnel entrance. Stepping past him, Trapper climbed through the newly-formed crater that spanned the room. Gameknight followed close behind the young woman, placing a torch near the dark opening to allow everyone to see. As he stepped into the passage, he glanced up at the quartz teeth that hung overhead and shuddered.

"I have a bad feeling about this," Hunter said behind him.

Gameknight glanced over his shoulder at her and tried to give her an encouraging smile, but all he could muster was an uncertain grimace.

I know the feeling, he thought to himself.

Gameknight knew they had no choice. Herobrine's timer was somewhere down in these tunnels, and nothing was going to stop him from reaching it. He only hoped they could get there in time before everything and everyone was destroyed.

CHAPTER 21

SKELETONS

The explosion rumbled through the rock around them. Reaper glanced up at the walls of the massive cavern, wondering if they would hold or if a thousand blocks of stone and sand were about to fall down upon their bony heads.

But hold they did, and an evil smile spread across the skeleton king's pale face.

"It appearsssss we have vissssssitorsssss," the spider queen said. "Perhapssss I sssshould recall my sssspiderssss from outsssssside."

"No," Reaper snapped. "You said your spiders were patrolling around the base of the mountain, right?"

The queen of the spiders nodded her fuzzy black head.

"Leave them there. This may just be a single NPC or user looking for adventure. Let your spider army continue to watch the base of the mountain so that the User-that-is-not-a-user will not reach the tunnel entrance. I will take care of the any intruders—that is, if any of them survive long enough to find me."

Reaper reached into his inventory and drew his longbow. He turned and peered into the dark shadows that surrounded the edge of the cobblestone platform on which they stood. Slowly, he raised his bow high overhead, signaling to his troops. Seeing the command, a hundred skeletons stepped out of the darkness and moved to the center of the platform, each with a deadly bow in their pale fists, arrows notched.

"I will personally deploy my skeletons throughout the tunnels that burrow deep into this mountain," the king of the skeletons said. "We will plug every tunnel with my warriors so that the intruders will be denied entrance to this sacred cave. If it is the User-that-is-not-a-user, then even better. He will not be allowed to interfere with Herobrine's command blocks."

The skeleton king strode out of the cavern with his army of monsters following close behind him, the clatter of their bones echoing off the walls.

They moved across the bridge that led from the cobblestone platform to the single opening in the side of the massive cavern. With no railing on the side of the bridge, the monsters slowed so as not to fall. They all knew that the darkness surrounding the bridge stretched all the way down to bedrock, and a fall would be a lethal mistake.

Once they were safely across, the skeletons spread out, moving farther into the tunnel to make room for the rest of the monster horde. Reaper, who had waited to cross the bridge last, pushed his way through the collection of bony creatures until he was at the head of the company. He then led his army through the complex labyrinth of passages. The tunnel split multiple times, each intersecting corridor leading in a different direction. Redstone torches adorned the walls here and there, casting just enough light to navigate the shadowy passages, yet still keeping the tunnel in darkness. The king of the skeletons left a squad of monsters at the mouth of every corridor, making sure his warriors protected every pathway to Herobrine's chamber.

"Hug the walls and stay in the shadows, my warriors," Reaper commanded to every group. "I'm sure the many traps hidden throughout the tunnels above us will destroy anyone that tries to get down here. But if they fail and the User-that-is-not-a-user shows his pathetic face, then one of you must come to Herobrine's chamber and report his presence, while the rest stay and engage him in glorious battle."

All of the skeletons looked eager to meet their enemy, but none more than Reaper. Notching an arrow to his longbow, he tested the sharpness of the arrowhead. The razor-sharp point scratched a deep line into his bony finger. He held the bow and arrow up over his head and laughed with evil glee.

"Soon, you will become very acquainted with this arrow, Gameknight999," Reaper said aloud to the echoing tunnel, then laughed a dry, hacking laugh, his lifeless eyes filled with hatred.

CHAPTER 22

THE CAVE OF DOOM

Trapper led the party slowly through the passages, a torch in one hand. She stared straight down as she moved cautiously forward, inspecting every inch of the tunnel's floor for pressure plates and tripwires. So far, Trapper had disarmed seven booby-traps, all of them similar in design and placement, which made them easier to spot.

As they moved along a straight section, a sound, barely audible, echoed off the stone walls.

"Everyone stop," Gameknight said in a hushed voice.

"Why are you whispering?" Hunter asked, her voice not so quiet.

"Shhh . . . there are monsters nearby," he replied. "Stand still and listen."

They all stood motionless and strained their ears for any noises echoing through the passage.

And then it happened again—a clattering sound, like someone was shaking a bag filled with old, dry sticks.

"Skeletons," Butch growled as he drew his iron sword.

A purple glow filled the tunnel when Hunter and Stitcher drew their own enchanted weapons. In the dimly-lit tunnel, the additional light seemed bright . . . and too obvious. It would make them much easier to see, Gameknight realized.

"Everyone, put away your enchanted weapons and magical armor," the User-that-is-not-a-user said. "The light they're giving off will give us away too soon. We need the cover of darkness to get close and retain the element of surprise."

"But I need a torch to see if there are any traps ahead," Trapper said.

"We haven't come across a trap for a while," Gameknight replied after he thought for a moment. "There certainly can't be any traps near the skeletons. The clumsy monsters would set them off and be destroyed." He looked down at the young NPC and shrugged. "We'll just have to risk it."

Gameknight quietly took off his enchanted diamond armor and replaced it with a set of dull iron. He then drew his iron sword and red shield and moved on through the tunnel. The sound of clattering bones grew louder as he went forward. Clearly, there were skeletons ahead, but it did not sound as if it were a large group. Ahead, the tunnel curved to the left. The sound was coming from just around that corner.

Moving as quietly as possible, Gameknight stepped up to the rocky bend, then peered around it. In the intersection of two tunnels, he saw a collection of skeletons just barely visible in the light of a nearby redstone torch. The monsters seemed to be trying to hide in the darkness near the torch, but too many were foolishly standing near the light. As a result, he could see at least four of the creatures. Likely there were just as many close by, hiding in the shadows.

Pulling his head back, the User-that-is-not-a-user turned and faced his friends.

"There are skeletons ahead, as we thought," Gameknight said. "It isn't clear how many, as I'd bet some are probably hiding in the darkness. Here's what we're going to do."

Gameknight999 explained his plan. Once everyone knew their jobs, the User-that-is-not-a-user drew his iron sword and shield, then readied himself for battle.

"Everyone ready?" he asked.

The NPCs all nodded their blocky heads.

"OK, Digger, Butch, let's go," Gameknight said. "Crafter, wait ten seconds, then follow with the rest."

"OK," replied his friend.

Gripping his sword firmly, Gameknight dashed around the corner and headed straight for the monsters, his shield held before him, Digger and Butch one step behind.

His footsteps betrayed his presence before he reached the light of the redstone torch. Arrows bounced off his shield as he charged forward. Not bothering to watch where he was running, Gameknight smashed through the skeletons without slowing, then continued down the corridor. After four blocks, he skidded to a stop, then turned to face the monsters.

Gameknight tossed his shield up to Butch, who was now closest to the skeletons. With sharp missiles bouncing off their defenses, they slowly but steadily advanced. Gameknight moved to Butch's right, while Digger went to the left.

Crafter then appeared out of the darkness with the rest of the army, attacking the skeletons from behind. They fell on the monsters with such ferocity that the skeletons had no choice but to take a step back to regain their balance. Now surrounded, the NPCs tore into the monster formation, carving a path of destruction through the mob. As the bones and XP began to fill the floor, one of the skeletons dropped its bow and fled into the darkness.

"Herder, don't let that monster get away!" Gameknight shouted.

"Wolves, attack!" Herder yelled.

A dozen furry white blurs streaked into the darkness, their growls filling the air. The clatter of bones sounded, then everything was silent. The wolves trotted back a minute later, a look of majestic pride on their faces.

"Try to keep one alive," Gameknight reminded his army, as the mob shrank smaller and smaller.

Finally, only one remained. Somehow, Hunter managed to knock the bow from its grip, leaving the skeleton with only an arrow to defend itself. Slowly, the NPCs closed in, surrounding the lone defender.

"You can answer our questions, and live," Gameknight said as he pushed through the crowd. "Or you can perish."

When he reached the front of the group, the skeleton looked surprised when it saw the letters floating over Gameknight's head.

"The enemy is here," the skeleton hissed.

"Apparently you're famous," Hunter said with a smile.

The skeleton jumped at Gameknight, holding the arrow like a dagger, but before it could make contact, Butch slammed into the creature with the shield. The monster flashed red as the collision took more of its HP, leaving it barely alive. The skeleton crumbled to the floor.

"Now I will say again: you can answer our questions and live, or be destroyed," the User-that-is-not-a-user said.

"It does not matter," the skeleton said. "We are prepared for you and your villagers. The enemy will never set foot inside of Herobrine's chamber. Our skeletons are ready at every entrance. You don't stand a chance."

"He's a chatty one," Hunter said with a grin.

"Hunter, shush," Stitcher chided.

"I was hoping to fight some spiders down here. You skeletons are too easy to pose any real challenge," Gameknight goaded.

"Shaivalak has something waiting for you down there that will destroy you and all your pathetic NPCs," the skeleton rasped. "At the flick of a switch, she will crush all of you. But you will never get near enough for her to use that block. Our skeletons will stop you. A group this large could never get into Herobrine's chamber without being seen."

"We'll see about that, skeleton," Gameknight said with a smile. "Thank you for the information, though."

The monster glared at the User-that-is-not-a-user, his eyes burning with hatred. With the last bit of his strength, the monster lunged at Gameknight999. But before it could reach him, two flaming arrows streaked through the air and destroyed the creature.

"I knew the skeleton was going to try something like that," Hunter said from the right side of the tunnel.

"Me, too," Stitcher added from the left.

"You heard what he said about the spider queen switching a block on," Crafter said. "It matches what the spider said. They must have meant a command block."

"But how can they use a block to cause spiders to appear?" Digger asked.

"Command blocks can be used to do incredible things in Minecraft," Gameknight explained. "Spawning monsters is a relatively easy task. Maybe that's what the spider has, a command block that will either create or teleport her minions to her."

"That sounds bad," Butch said.

"It does indeed," Crafter replied.

"But the skeleton give us even more information," Gameknight added. "He said that a large party could not sneak their way into the chamber. That means two things. One: there is a chamber that we must find, and two: a small party *could* sneak in."

"But where *is* the chamber?" Crafter asked.

"I think I know the answer to that question," said a voice from the darkness.

Trapper stepped out from the tunnel that continued leading downward, further into the depths of the mountain. Her blonde hair glowed a warm orange when she entered into the light of the redstone torch.

"While all of you were doing your fighting thing, I went forward and explored a little," she said. "A little way down this tunnel, there is a hole in the wall that opens to a massive cavern. Come see."

Without waiting for anyone to respond, she turned and ran off into the darkness. Gameknight looked at Crafter and shrugged, then followed the girl, the rest of the NPCs following close behind. They followed the tunnel for maybe a minute when they came to a section that was missing a wall.

Gameknight moved along the wall and peered around the edge of the hole. Below was a massive cavern bigger than any zombie-town he'd ever seen. There was one entrance to the cave. He could see it was guarded by a small group of skeletons. Reaper stood nearby with his huge longbow made of bone in his right hand. There were no other monsters visible.

"That foolish skeleton king must have spread out his forces through all the tunnels," Butch said. "You never divide your forces. What was that idiot thinking?"

"You wish he had all his skeletons together?" Hunter asked.

Butch shook his head. "I'm glad he is a fool," the big NPC replied. "It will be that much easier for us."

"Gameknight, you see the numbers on the far end of the chamber?" Crafter said.

He glanced in the direction Crafter was pointing. Bright numbers made from redstone lanterns were visible on the dark wall, the number 18 shining bright. It dropped to 17 as they watched.

"That must be hooked up the timer circuit," Gameknight said as he fit the pieces of the puzzle together in his mind.

Crafter nodded, then reached into his inventory and pulled out a redstone torch. He placed it on the far wall, casting a dim crimson glow in the tunnel, allowing them to see each other a little better.

"Why didn't Herobrine have the thing just go off already?" Stitcher asked.

"I bet he's waiting until that pool beneath the display is filled," Gameknight said. "Notice the lava flowing out from that hole in the wall? I bet the timer is waiting until the pool is filled, then the command blocks will teleport the lava to all of the villages."

"We have to stop that timer," Digger said, his voice filled with rage. "But how do we get down there? You see that narrow bridge? Even a small group of skeletons could hold that bridge against a large force for a long time." He turned away from the cavern and looked at Gameknight999. "This is going to be difficult, if not impossible. We'll have to get past the skeletons in that chamber, then deal with the spider queen and her magical command block. Then we'd have to go to the far end of the cavern and destroy everything. I don't know how we're going to do it."

Crafter nodded, agreeing with Digger's summation.

Gameknight moved forward and peered down into the chamber again. As he stared at the cave and skeletons and bridge, the puzzle pieces started to tumble around in his head. He knew there was a solution here; he just had to see it.

I can't believe anyone would try to destroy all the lives on the server, just for spite, Gameknight thought. *This must be stopped. I'm responsible for this because I didn't stop Herobrine sooner. I cannot . . . no, I will not allow this to happen.*

"It sure would be convenient if this cavern had a back door," Hunter said. "Maybe we could just use that to sneak in and solve all our problems."

Suddenly an image of the obsidian pillars in The End flashed in his mind.

Of course . . . it worked then, it would have to work now. But what about the spider's command block?

One of the wolves nipped at Gameknight's ankle. He looked down at the animal and realized what the creature was thinking.

"Of course," the User-that-is-not-a-user said to the animal. "I'm sure that would work. I bet the Oracle told you to do that, didn't she?"

The music of Minecraft swelled in his mind as all the pieces of the plan came together, making him smile. The wolf panted happily.

"Oh no . . . Gameknight's started talking to himself," Hunter said. "Either he's going crazy, or he's figured it all out."

"Hunter, be quiet and let him think," Stitcher snapped.

Gameknight turned to the sisters and smiled.

"You *did* figure it out, didn't you?" Hunter asked.

He nodded.

"Is it dangerous?" Stitcher asked.

Gameknight nodded again.

"Insanely dangerous?" Hunter asked.

The User-that-is-not-a-user nodded and gave her a smile.

"I like it!" she exclaimed.

"OK," Gameknight said. "Let me tell you what I have in mind."

CHAPTER 23

TUNNELS

ameknight, Hunter, and Butch left their companions in the narrow tunnel, careful to make as little noise as possible as they disappeared into the darkness. The User-that-is-not-a-user looked back at their company. They were still clustered around the small opening that looked down into the massive chamber, the single redstone torch barely making them visible. Each was taking turns looking at the device of destruction that sat on the rocky floor below, waiting.

I hope my plan works and we can get into that cave without any of the skeletons knowing we're there, Gameknight thought. *We can't battle hundreds of skeletons with the few NPCs we have—that would be suicide.*

"Come on," Hunter whispered as she gently laid her hand on his shoulder. "The fun is down this way."

She moved like a ghost, dashing from shadow to shadow as she led the way through the descending passage, which twisted and turned as it bore deep into the stone and dirt. Gameknight held a red-stone torch to give a small amount of illumination so they could see any traps or tripwires, but found none. Likely, the traps were just near the entrance to the tunnel network; no one had expected them to make it this far.

Soon, they began to hear the sounds of clatter-ing bones, and knew they were getting close. Put-ting out the redstone torch, the trio approached slowly through the darkness, peering around rocky outcroppings and stone formations. Ahead was an intersection of two tunnels; one continuing down-ward while the other sloped upward. At the center of the crossing was a single redstone torch. It cast a pale red glow onto the tunnel walls and stone floor.

The tunnels looked empty.

But then something moved just at the edge of the circle of illumination, as a clattering sound reached the three intruders. Gameknight peered through the darkness, his eyes becoming accus-tomed to the pale light, and features began to emerge from the shadows. Pale skeletons stood in the darkness, their white bones reflecting just enough of the crimson light to be visible.

"There's a group of at least thirty skeletons up ahead," Hunter whispered.

"I don't think we can fight that many," Butch said, "not even if we had that boy's wolves with us."

Hunter stared at the monsters. She moved slowly to the right wall of the tunnel and gazed down the tunnel, then moved to the left and repeated the process. Then she turned and faced her friends, a smile just barely visible through the darkness.

"I can draw them off, I think," she said.

"How?" Gameknight asked.

She just looked at him and smiled again, then pulled out a block of dirt and placed it on the far right side of the tunnel. She stuck an arrow into the block so that it was easy to grab.

"I'll have to do this quick so they won't see my bow," Hunter said as she carefully placed more blocks of dirt throughout the passage, leaving only a narrow pass through which to shoot. Once she was satisfied with her work, she stood in her archer stance, but left her bow in her inventory.

"What are you doing?" Gameknight whispered.

"Waiting for the right time," she replied, "Now be quiet and let me do my thing."

Slowly, she reached into her inventory, then stood motionless and waited. Gameknight turned and looked at the skeletons. Apparently, the monsters had become bored with standing in the shadows. They all thought there was no way that an enemy could make it this far into the mountain, and they'd grown careless, congregating around the redstone torch and shuffling about aimlessly. The clattering of their bones filled the passage, the echoes making it sound as if there were a few hundred of the monsters standing before them instead of just thirty.

But then a new sound echoed off something, causing the skeletons to all look to one side. That was what Hunter was waiting for.

In a practiced, fluid movement, she pulled out her enchanted bow and notched the arrow in a blink of an eye. Drawing the arrow back, she fired it through the tunnel, then put away her bow before anyone saw the iridescent glow. The whole thing happened in a flash. The flaming projectile arched upward, narrowly missing the ceiling as it streaked through the air, then flew above the intersection without being seen and darted into the adjacent upward-sloping passage. The flaming arrow stuck into the ground far into the ascending passage, the magical flame still burning.

The skeletons just stood there, unmoving and confused. They hadn't even noticed.

"It didn't work," grumbled Butch quietly.

"Wait for it. Skeletons aren't very smart," Hunter whispered.

And then it happened; one of the skeletons saw the burning arrow and pointed. The other monsters looked up the passage, then ran to investigate, leaving only one to guard the intersection.

"Now," Hunter said as she pulled out a normal bow and notched an arrow.

Drawing his iron sword, Gameknight adjusted his non-magical iron armor and followed his friend as she leapt forward with the silent grace of a predatory cat. Streaking noiselessly from shadow to shadow, they closed in on the foolish monster that had stayed behind, his bony back still to them. When they were at the edge of the light cast by the redstone torch, Butch reached out and wrapped his strong arms around the monster, placing a hand over his mouth. At the same time, Hunter fired her arrows at the creature, aiming precisely between the butcher's muscular arms. In seconds, it disappeared without a sound, the monster's HP consumed. Gameknight moved forward and snatched up the XP and bones, then ran to the passage that angled downward, toward their goal, leaving behind an empty intersection with no trace that they'd ever been there.

They repeated this process of drawing off the foolish skeletons with a flaming arrow, then streaking by the unprotected intersection. After they had tricked their way through three additional intersections, the trio finally found themselves at the entrance to Herobrine's chamber.

Peering into the huge opening, Gameknight could clearly see the details of the chamber now. There was a narrow strip of rock that stretched out into the cavern, the darkness of a fatal drop wrapping around both sides. At the end of the narrow bridge was a huge stone circle that extended from the left side of the massive cave to the right but did not extend to the far wall where the glowing numbers were slowly ticking down. Instead, it only covered the near half of the cavern, with another narrow bridge extending to a second platform of stone that was hidden in shadow. Across that far, stony plane, he could see some kind of blocks in the shadows, but the darkness made them difficult to identify. Clearly, these bridges were designed so that monsters on the stone platforms could defend themselves easily, holding the narrow bridge and keeping intruders from advancing.

Gameknight smiled.

Your bridge won't stop us, Herobrine, Gameknight thought. *Apparently, you didn't think of everything, did you?*

He smiled to himself.

"You look like an idiot," Hunter whispered. "What are you smiling about?"

"Oh, nothing," the User-that-is-not-a-user replied.

At the other end of the bridge, a cluster of skeletons were standing about, not paying attention to anything. In the dim light of the redstone torches, Gameknight could see a small hole high up on the wall to the right side, a subtle glow of red light marking its position. Then he noticed a single command block on the platform near the left wall, a lever placed to its side. *It must be the spider queen's command block*, he thought. *That's my target.*

"You two ready?" Gameknight asked.

They both nodded.

"Then let's get this thing done."

I hope this works, he thought as he pulled out a block of cobblestone and placed it on the sheer wall of the cavern, using it as a ledge, then inched out onto it as Hunter and Butch did the same on the opposite side. They slowly moved along the perimeter of the cavern wall, standing precariously on a single block of stone, while what seemed like an endless drop yawned below them.

Suppressing his fear, he placed the next block on the side of the wall. The single cube of cobblestone seemed barely wide enough to hold him, and he had to remind himself over and over that he wouldn't fall. That massive drop beneath him made everything seem small and insignificant. Gameknight felt momentarily paralyzed with fear as he stared down into the shadows.

I can do this, he thought as he pulled his gaze away from the darkness beneath him. Gameknight took a tentative step forward. Pulling another block of stone from his inventory, he stuck the cube against the cave wall and moved forward yet another step, his eyes focused on his target, the lone command block.

I really hope this works, Gameknight thought, *or I'll cause the deaths of all these people, including my friends.*

He shuddered at the thought and tried to push it away, but the uncertainty seemed to swell within his mind.

If only I'd stopped Herobrine sooner, the familiar voice of guilt said within his mind.

CHAPTER 24
REALIZATION

Gameknight999 hugged the smooth cavern wall, trying not to breathe. A skeleton was approaching below. The bony monster moved along the edge of the cobblestone platform, coming closer and closer. Walking up to the edge, the monster looked down into the seemingly endless darkness, then stepped away from the precipice. He hadn't thought to look up at the wall, where the User-that-is-not-a-user stood flattened against the wall on a single block ledge.

Gameknight's foot had slipped moments earlier, and the noise drew the attention of the guard. If the monster saw him, he was in serious trouble.

Staying perfectly still, the User-that-is-not-a-user tried to slow his heartbeat. The rhythmic pounding of his heart sounded incredibly loud within his chest and he was afraid maybe the skeleton would hear it.

The monster looked around, then glanced up at the large numbers at the far end of the cavern. The number 13 shone bright in the darkness, which made the skeleton smile. Turning back, the creature shuffled away, satisfied that there was nothing to see.

Gameknight999 slowly exhaled, then took a calming breath as his heartbeat slowed to a normal pace. He could feel tiny square beads of sweat forming on his forehead and running down his face. They stung as the little cubes made it into his eyes, but he ignored the discomfort and concentrated on the task at hand. Pulling out another cobblestone block, he placed it on the sheer wall and moved forward another step, slowly making his way around the perimeter of the huge cavern. His target, the lone command block, was still a few blocks out of reach, but he was getting closer.

On the other side of the cavern, he could barely see Hunter and Butch, but every now and then a glint of red light would reflect off someone's armor, showing him their progress. They were almost to the far section of the cobblestone platform and would soon be moving to Phase II; he had to hurry up with his task.

Placing the blocks faster, Gameknight moved along the narrow ledge he was building. The ticking numbers on the other side of the gigantic cavern made him want to hurry, but he knew any misstep would mean his death; he had to be careful.

Placing more cobblestone, he was soon nearly in reach of the command block. For safety's sake, he stuck two more blocks against the sheer wall and moved closer to the checkered orange cube. It was now within reach.

Crouching, Gameknight stretched out a hand and set it on the block. Closing his eyes, he imagined he was at his computer, as he had done many times while within the game. Focusing his mind on the mouse he liked to use, he imagined himself moving the cursor over the command block. With every fiber of his being, he tried to right click the command block with his mind. Instantly, a series of letters appeared in his mind, and Gameknight was shocked at what he saw. The command block, when activated, was programmed to make a hundred spiders and fifty cave spiders appear on the platform. If Shaivalak had flipped that lever, the NPCs would have been doomed.

He tried to erase the command, but for some reason, he couldn't.

Well, if I can't delete the command, then let's see if I can change it, Gameknight thought.

Reaching out with his mind, Gameknight focused on his mouse and imagined part of the command highlighted, then replaced some of the item numbers with another that he knew well. But would this new command take effect? Gameknight999 wasn't sure. All he could do was hope that he'd done it right.

Just then, the User-that-is-not-user heard a splashing sound on the other side of the chamber. All of the skeletons near the narrow bridge turned toward the sound, curious to see what it was. But none would venture too far into the darkness; bravery was not a skeleton's strongest characteristic.

An iridescent purple glow formed on the opposite side of the cavern, revealing Hunter and Butch standing knee deep in water. Drawing an arrow, Hunter fired it straight up into the air. The projectile instantly burst aflame when it left her bow, streaking through the air like a feathery meteor.

"NPCs!" one of the skeletons yelled. "There are NPCs in the chamber!"

Hunter spun and fired an arrow at the outspoken skeleton, then followed the shot with two more, silencing the squad leader and leaving his bones scattered on the ground. But it was too late. Two skeletons were already running across the bridge to gather more forces, too far away to silence.

A loud splash sounded near Hunter. Gameknight watched as villagers jumped out of the opening high up on the cave wall. They plummeted at least thirty blocks until they landed in the water that Butch and Hunter had spread across the stone platform, the liquid cushioning their fall. Once they landed, the NPCs waded out and immediately began building fortifications out of stone and dirt. Leaning out from behind blocks of cobblestone, they fired on the skeletons that were rushing toward them, keeping the small squad of monsters from approaching.

A noise that sounded like a million sticks clattering together echoed through the chamber. Reaper, the king of the skeletons, ran across the narrow bridge with at least a hundred skeletons following close behind. Gameknight had to get to the other end of the bridge to stop that mob!

Removing his iron armor, he quickly replaced it with his enchanted diamond armor. There was no sense in staying hidden any longer. Then he drew his diamond sword with his right hand and his shield with his left. Sprinting with all his speed, Gameknight charged at the skeletons, his battle cry echoing through the chamber.

"FOR MINECRAFT!"

The echo made it sound as if he had fifty warriors behind him, which caused the bony creatures to pause in fear for just a moment, which was all Gameknight needed. Charging into the small group of skeletons on their side of the bridge, he smashed into one with his shield, then landed three quick hits. The creature disappeared with a pop. He hoped the NPCs would take care of the other skeletons while Gameknight faced the bridge.

CLANK!

An arrow bounced off his shield. Turning toward the sound, Gameknight found the skeleton king drawing another arrow, the razor-sharp point aimed directly at his head. The User-that-is-not-a-user brought up his shield just in time to deflect the projectile harmlessly away.

"You are a fool for coming here, User-that-is-not-a-user," the skeleton king rasped.

"We'll see who the fool really is," Gameknight replied.

He moved toward the end of the bridge, but before he could reach it, pain exploded across his back. Spinning quickly, he found two skeletons facing him, their bows empty. They each drew another arrow, but before they could fire, Gameknight charged, his shield held out in front of him. Another arrow stuck him in his back, causing more pain to radiate through his body like fire. Hacking laughter came from the bridge. Gameknight knew it was Reaper.

I can't stay here. There are too many skeletons nearby, Gameknight thought.

"Gameknight, get back here, NOW!" Hunter yelled from the newly-constructed fortification.

Spinning around, the User-that-is-not-a-user steadily walked backward, careful not to trip and fall, while deadly missiles struck his shield. Hunter and Stitcher stepped to his side and fired at the nearest of the skeletons, driving them back, allowing Gameknight to turn and run. In seconds, they were all safely behind the barricade.

"What were you thinking?" Hunter asked as she pulled the many arrows out of his shield.

"Ahh . . . well . . . I was . . ."

"You weren't thinking, that was the problem," she said.

"The timer, look!" Crafter exclaimed.

All the NPCs turned and looked up at the glowing display on the far side of the cavern. The number clicked from 11 to 10. The redstone lamp that sat near the spewing lava beat relentlessly, pulsing out the cadence to its inevitable end.

"We must hurry," Butch said. "I can see there is another narrow bridge leading to the dark section of the cavern. There are blocks all across the floor; those must be the command blocks."

"Let's get over there and break up all the redstone," Digger said.

There are too many of them," Gameknight said. "We'll never get them all."

"But at least we can save some of the villages," Crafter said.

"Oh no . . . it's too late," Stitcher said. "Look!"

Another fifty skeletons emerged from the shadows and crossed the bridge that led to the command blocks. Now all of the skeletons had crossed over onto the cobblestone platform. They were surrounded.

"This is turning out to be a really great plan," Hunter said to Gameknight as she fired an arrow at a skeleton.

Gameknight sighed.

Then a clicking sound echoed off the cavern walls. Near the lone command block, a dark shape climbed around the edge of the platform from underneath it and moved out into the light. Multiple bright purple eyes shone in the darkness, each filled with hatred and a desire to destroy.

"You sssshould not have come here, Gameknght999," Shaivalak said. "You are a fool for tempting my patience."

"I will stop at nothing to protect the NPCs of Minecraft," Gameknight shouted back, trying to sound assertive. But his voice cracked with fear.

The skeletons laughed.

"You sound really confident," Reaper said as he moved across the platform and stood at the spider queen's side.

"Thissss isss Herobrine'ssss chamber, and you have no place here," Shaivalak said. "But at leasssst you will get to watch hisss revenge happen in persssson."

"We will stop you, somehow, spider," Gameknight said. His voice sounded even weaker.

The spider queen laughed.

"By defying Herobrine, you caussssed thissss fate for the villagerssss of Minecraft," the spider queen said. "You and you alone will be ressssponsible for their deathssss."

"No," Gameknight pleaded. "This can't be happening."

His voice weakened as his legs began to shake. He looked around at all the skeletons that surrounded them, and he knew they were completely outnumbered. They had no avenue of escape and no hope of surviving this battle.

Glancing up at the timer, he watched the display click to 9. Time was running out.

"Herobrine alwayssss told ussss you were a coward," the spider queen said, her eyes glowing bright with hatred. "The Maker'ssss device here and hissss actionsssss in the passsst have proven it. He hassss defined you to be a coward, and now hissss prediction hassss come true."

"No . . ." Gameknight pleaded, but then something in the Shaivalak's words struck a nerve.

His actions do not define me, he thought. *Only I can define myself. His actions defined the kind of monster* he *truly was, not me.*

Gameknight drew his diamond sword and stepped over the barricade to stand out in the open.

"No. That monster does not define the kind of person I am," the User-that-is-not-a-user said. "Only my actions and choices define me."

He stood a little taller.

Crafter was right. This is not my fault; it's Herobrine's, Gameknight thought. *I did everything I could, and we ended up destroying that monster in our basement . . . at least I think I did? But I know one thing for sure: I didn't build this command block contraption, and I didn't start the timer; he did. And I refuse to let it continue!*

But what if Herobrine is still alive in Minecraft? A stray thought, one of his many fears, spoke up in the back of his mind.

"No, I saw the computer destroyed," he whispered softly to himself. "I saw the hard drive and computer chips shattered into a million pieces. If Herobrine were still in Minecraft, he would have shown his gloating face by now. That evil virus would have tried to amplify my guilt and would want to revel in my despair. No . . . Herobrine must be gone."

It sounded like a plea. He tried to push away his fears, but the uncertainty of Herobrine's fate still hid in the shadowy corners of his mind like a persistent nightmare.

"No," the User-that-is-not-a-user said in a strong voice. "I am in command of my own destiny, and I say NO MORE!"

Bravery flowed through his body as he thought of all the things he'd done and all the NPCs he'd helped. He always chose the path that would help the most people, and the User-that-is-not-a-user realized he was proud of that fact.

As the courage pushed away the feelings of guilt and uncertainty, Gameknight glared at the spider queen, then drew his iron sword and took another step closer. The skeletons wanted to attack, but the spider queen held up a claw, holding back the bony creatures.

"I am the User-that-is-not-a-user, protector of Minecraft, and my fate is my own to define, not your pathetic Maker's," Gameknight said, his voice filled with confidence. It echoed off the stone walls and sounded as if it were coming at them from all sides.

"You wordsss are weak, jusssst like Herobrine alwayssss ssssaid," spat Shaivalak. "My only wisssssh issss that the Maker were here to witnesssss your desssstruction."

"Oh, really?" Gameknight replied. "You miss your precious Maker?"

The echoes of uncertainty that still bounced around in his mind all vaporized as the truth surfaced within his head. Herobrine *was* gone! He glanced at Crafter behind him. The young NPC's unibrow was raised with curiosity as revelation showed on his face.

"If he were here, he would desssstroy you himssssself," the spider queen hissed. "But he issss taking hissss revenge on the physsssical world."

Gameknight laughed.

"Your precious Maker never made it to the Internet. We trapped him in a puny little computer, then destroyed it with an old, rusty hammer." He paused for a moment, then gave the spider queen a smile. "Do you think I could come back into Minecraft if Herobrine were destroying the physical world? Would I have time to come play a computer game?"

"No!" she cried. "He issss desssstroying the physsssical world assss we sssspeak. He ssssaid he would, and then he wassss going to bring ussss into that world with him."

"*Now* look who is being the fool," Gameknight said with a smile. "I deleted Herobrine like an old, useless program that served no purpose. Everything about him is gone, as if he never existed."

Shaivalak's eyes glowed bright purple, filled with hate. They lit the chamber with a lavender hue that allowed Gameknight to see the massive field of command blocks on the next platform.

"You think everything about Herobrine is gone?" the spider queen asked. "Well then, let me sssshow you what he left for you . . . a sssspecial pressssent dedicated to this moment; our meeting again."

Reaching up, she placed one of her wicked curved claws on the lever next to the command block and pushed. It moved slowly at first, then clicked in place, activating the redstone around the orange-checkered cube.

The air between Gameknight999 and Shaivalak began to shimmer and sparkle. Then a hundred creatures appeared . . . and the User-that-is-not-a-user gasped as hundreds of red eyes stared up at him.

CHAPTER 25

SHAIVALAK

Wolves, by the hundreds, stared up at Gameknight999. Their fur was bristling with anger as their tails stuck straight out like white daggers. It was clear these wolves were really, really angry; they could sense their ancient enemy, the skeletons, were nearby. As one, the wolves turned and fell on the monsters. They surged forward, running straight at the skeletons and attacking with powerful jaws, snapping and tearing into the mob with merciless fury.

"YEAH!" Hunter shouted as she fired her flaming arrows at the skeletons. Stitcher did the same.

"You did it!" Crafter yelled over the growling animals. "You changed the command block! The spider queen didn't get the monsters she expected."

"And look at her," Digger added. "She looks a little upset."

The spider queen's eyes blazed bright purple and filled with hatred.

Just then, one of the wolves yelped in pain as an arrow pierced its side.

"No you don't!" Herder screamed.

The lanky boy jumped over the fortifications and charged forward with an outstretched iron sword. This triggered the rest of the NPCs to charge with weapons drawn, smashing into the skeletons.

The spider queen glared at Gameknight, her rage filling every one of her blazing eyes.

"What did you do to the Maker'ssss command block?" she hissed.

"I reprogrammed it," Gameknight shouted. "You don't become the King of the Griefers without knowing how to use command blocks." He smiled at his foe.

A wolf saw Shaivalak and attacked. The spider queen darted to the side, then reached out with her wicked, curved claws. The sharp points tore at the poor animal's HP until it disappeared with a yelp.

"No, you leave them alone!" Herder screamed, then charged at the spider.

"Herder, NO!" Gameknight said, but it was too late.

Herder ran at the monster, his iron sword outstretched. Gameknight knew the boy had little skill with the blade, so his only choice was to dash forward and get to the monster first.

"FOR MINECRAFT!" he shouted and charged straight at the spider.

Shaivalak turned away from Herder and ran straight at Gameknight999. They both jumped into the air and smashed into each other. The spider's claws scratched into Gameknight's already weakened armor, digging deep grooves into its shiny surface. The User-that-is-not-a-user tried to swing his diamond sword at the spider, but one of her back claws deflected the blow. They landed in a heap and quickly separated.

"You have interfered with the Maker'ssss planssss," the spider queen hissed. "Hissss commandssss were clear. We are to punissssh everyone that oppossssed him. His great device will dessssstroy all living creaturessss."

"Not if I stop you first," Gameknight growled.

Darting forward, the User-that-is-not-a-user slashed at the monster with his iron blade, then drove his diamond sword forward. He hit one of her legs, making her flash red, but quickly, the spider counterattacked, driving her claws deep into his diamond leggings.

Gameknight screamed out in pain as a sharp claw found flesh.

Not waiting an instant, he charged forward again, bringing both blades down in what should have been a killing blow, but Shaivalak was too fast. She was smaller than her predecessor, Shaikulud, but much faster. Gameknight's blades found empty air as he smashed into the cobblestone floor. Rolling to the side, he narrowly avoided a claw to his head, but as he rose, the User-that-is-not-a-user found his right foot stuck in a spider's web.

"Today issss the day you will be dessssstroyed," the spider queen said.

"Just like the former queen, you talk too much," Gameknight spat.

With both his swords, he chopped at the web, cutting through it with two hits. Moving to the right, he circled his opponent, looking for any weakness to exploit.

"The Maker ssssaid you would be here when the device activated," Shaivalak said. "He left a messssssage for you. He ssssaid, if you hadn't opposssssed him, he would have sssspared the villagerssss. He ssssaid the blame for all thissss fallssss upon you."

Gameknight heard the words and could just imagine Herobrine saying them. That AI virus had a way of manipulating his enemy's emotions, and he was still doing it from the grave, like some kind of phantom. He knew it was all just a game to Herobrine, but still heard the truth in the words.

"And when I am done with you, I'm going to torture that lanky boy over there, and it will all be your fault," the spider queen said. "You have forced me to do thissss, and the blame will be yourssss. It will be like you are doing the killing when my clawssss do their damage."

The music of Minecraft suddenly swelled and filled Gameknight's mind, the lyrical tones driving away his doubts and fear, leaving only courage and truth in their place.

"Your words do not bother me, spider," the User-that-is-not-a-user said. "I know now that I control my own fate, just as you control yours. If you lay a single claw on my friends, it will be because you have chosen to do so. And you *will* be held accountable."

Gameknight circled to the left, trying to see where the skeleton king had gone, but it was as if he had disappeared into the shadows. Just then, the clicking sound of spiders echoed off the walls as half-a-dozen of the monsters climbed down the walls and joined the fray.

"You see, my minionssss have finally arrived," the spider queen said. "My great army of sssssisterssss will come and dessssstroy all of you."

Gameknight laughed.

"You know nothing," he said. "That is all that is left of your army. We destroyed nearly all of them. Your six spiders are all that will come to your aid." He took a step forward and lowered his diamond sword to the ground. "It's over. Just surrender and stop the violence."

"Never!" Shaivalak spat.

She charged forward, but Gameknight was ready. He rolled to his right, then brought up his iron sword as she soared overhead. Its sharp tip tore HP from the monster, making her flash red.

Standing, Gameknight turned to face his opponent and brought up his diamond sword just in time to block one of her claws from striking his chest. But he did not stop the other claw from raking across his leg. He flashed red with pain and stepped back to regain his bearings.

Bringing both swords up, he readied for another attack. But instead of charging forward, the spider shot out cubes of spider webs, trapping Gameknight's feet. As he swung his swords at the sticky filament, the spider's claw raked across his back.

Pain erupted along his arm. He tried to roll away, but his feet were still glued to the ground.

Another block of white web shot through the air and captured his left hand, trapping the iron sword in the sticky strands. Gameknight swung his diamond sword at the web, slowly cutting through the strands, but another block of web appeared, making the task harder.

More pain exploded through his body as another claw found a gap between armored plates.

"You don't look sssso fierce to me now," Shaivalak hissed.

She attacked again, this time dragging her claw across Gameknight's leg. His diamond coating shattered as the curved claw destroyed the last of the diamond legging's strength.

"Now I will do what my predecessssssor failed to do: desssstroy Gameknight999," the spider queen said as she stood directly in front of him. With her eyes glowing bright with rage, she charged forward.

The sound of two voices echoed through the cave.

"FOR GAMEKNIGHT999!" they cried as two flaming arrows streaked through the air, flying directly over Gameknight's shoulders. The missiles zoomed so close to his head that his hair was singed. The arrows struck the spider, pushing her back. Then another pair of arrows flew, zipping past his ears, hitting her again. A look of shock and fear filled her purple eyes as the last pair of arrows hit her in the chest, consuming the last of her HP. With a look of surprise in her multiple eyes, she disappeared.

Shaivalak, the spider queen, was gone.

CHAPTER 26

REAPER

"The timers!" Crafter yelled.

Gameknight turned and looked at the display on the wall. It was down to 8. There was no time to celebrate.

He quickly chopped through the rest of the spiderweb that had him immobilized, then ran through the battlefield. With his two swords, he carved a path through the skeletons, sometimes just smashing into them with a lowered shoulder, sometimes kicking them out of the way. He streaked toward the shadowy side of the cavern and the narrow bridge that led to the sea of command blocks. But when he reached the bridge, a pale figure moved out onto the opposite end, emerging from the shadows like a ghostly apparition.

"You may have been able to dispatch that foolish spider," Reaper said from the shadows. "But now you must face me and my new pet."

The skeleton slowly moved out of the darkness. His pale bones became quickly visible, but strangely, his legs didn't seem to be moving.

"You have been a nuisance for too long, Gameknight999. It is now time for you to be destroyed."

As the skeleton king moved forward out of the shadows, Gameknight thought he saw eight points of red light moving beneath his body. They bobbed left and right while Reaper approached, but Gameknight still couldn't tell what it was. As the skeleton king moved into the dim light cast by a nearby redstone torch, eight fuzzy black legs materialized out of the shadows under him.

Gameknight was shocked. He was riding a spider. Reaper was now a spider jockey!

Gameknight had heard of these on the Internet, but had never battled one. People said they were difficult to fight; the skeleton's bow struck at you when you were far away, and the curved claws of the spider hit you when you were near. He shook with fear when he looked at the monstrous duo, then glanced at the timer on the far wall. The number changed from 7 to 6. Pushing away his uncertainty, Gameknight999 glared at the monster.

"Herobrine is destroyed and his destructive influence on the villagers of the Overworld is over," Gameknight said. "The command blocks that stand behind you are all that is left of his evil ways."

"So you think, User-that-is-not-a-user." Reaper laughed, and gave him a knowing smile that made Gameknight999 wonder.

Is *this the last of Herobrine's tricks?* he thought.

"But enough talk. It is time for you to meet your doom," the skeleton king rasped.

The spider jockey charged forward across the narrow bridge that led to the command blocks, then stopped in the middle, denying anyone the ability to pass. The sharp blade of the skeleton's arrowhead scraped across Gameknight's shoulder as it streaked by, just narrowly missing him. Rolling under the next shot, Gameknight raced out onto the skinny bridge. He brought his swords forward, slicing at the spider's head. The giant monster backed up a step, then hissed as her eyes glowed bright red with hatred. Jumping into the air, Gameknight sliced at the skeleton. His attack was not meant to score a hit; he just intended to keep the bony creature off balance. When he landed on the ground, the User-that-is-not-a-user brought his dual swords down on the spider's shoulders, making the creature screech with pain as it flashed red. Before they could respond, Gameknight swung his swords wildly. The monstrous duo backed up quickly, inching a little closer to the command blocks, giving Reaper time to notch and fire another arrow. The projectile hit Gameknight in the side, causing pain to erupt throughout his body.

"Gameknight," a voice boomed from behind. He glanced over his shoulder and found Digger running across the cobblestone platform, a concerned look on his blocky face.

"Spleef," he shouted, then tossed his iron pickaxe into the air.

Understanding his plan, Gameknight dropped his iron sword and reached out for the tool. His sword clattered to the cobblestone bridge, then fell over the side, pinwheeling into the darkness. Glancing at the timer, he saw that it was now at 5. Catching the iron tool in his left hand, the User-that-is-not-a-user slowly advanced. The sword finally hit the ground with a clang, and the sound verified what Gameknight999 already knew in his gut: a fall from this height would be a death sentence.

Reaper fired again, but Gameknight was able to easily bat the arrow away with the pickaxe. He moved closer, then dug up one of the cobblestone blocks.

"If you think that is going to protect you, then the zombie king named you correctly, Fool," Reaper said.

The pair were still far from the missing block. He had to get them closer.

Gameknight stepped to the edge of the missing block, then put away his sword and shifted the pickaxe to his right hand. Reaper fired again, but the arrow was easily deflected.

"Come closer, coward," Gameknight said.

Reaper laughed.

"I am not a fool," the skeleton said, then launched two arrows at him in quick succession. Gameknight deflected the first arrow with a flick of his wrist, but the second arrow landed in his leg, causing his HP to drop dangerously low.

I have to get them closer, Gameknight thought.

"You know, Reaper, the spider queen begged for mercy just before I killed her," Gameknight lied. The spider stopped backing up and glared at him. "She said she knew her forces were weak and gutless, but in general, all spiders are cowards anyway. Look around you. None of them were even brave enough to come protect her."

The spider beneath Reaper clicked her mandibles together, the multiple eyes glowing bright red.

"And just before she died, you know what she said?" the User-that-is-not-a-user continued.

"Be quiet!" Reaper yelled. "You speak lies."

"The spider queen said she wished she'd been born an idiotic creeper so she could detonate herself and end her miserable, pathetic, useless life and stop being embarrassed by her own spiders."

"No one sssspeaks of Shaivalak that way," the spider hissed behind clicking mandibles.

"When she begged for her life, she kissed my feet and called me her Maker," Gameknight said with a smile.

"No . . . NO!" the sister shouted.

"Hold your position," Reaper commanded, but the spider was out of control.

She charged forward, her multiple red eyes glowing bright with hatred.

I have to time this just right or I'm dead, Gameknight thought.

The spider surged across the narrow cobblestone bridge. When she neared the broken section, she readied a leap. But before she could launch herself into the air, Gameknight used Digger's pickaxe and tore at the block in front of them. The huge monster instantly realized what her enemy was going to do and skidded to a halt, but she had already started to jump, and her momentum continued to carry her forward.

Ignoring the skeleton king, Gameknight smashed at the cobblestone block, striking again and again until the cracks that spread across its surface finally claimed the cube, causing it to crumble to dust. Scrambling to grab the edge of the block behind her, the spider started to tumble into the emptiness that surrounded the bridge.

Gameknight could hear her claws scraping against the hard stone, but they could not find purchase. Her screams mixed with Reaper's as the monsters tumbled off the bridge and were swallowed by the darkness.

Reaper, the king of the skeletons, was destroyed.

CHAPTER 27

HEROBRINE'S REVENGE

Sweat trickled down his square forehead. Wiping his brow with his free hand, Gameknight looked up at the timer display. It now showed 4. He had to hurry.

Pulling a block of cobblestone from his inventory, he placed it on the broken bridge where the spider had fallen through. Placing a second one, he ran across the bridge. Gameknight quickly found himself among hundreds of command blocks, all of them connected by lines of redstone powder. With a torch in his hand, Gameknight raced through the collection of orange-checkered blocks, looking for that one block that would control them all, and in the darkness, bind them.

"It must be here, somewhere," Gameknight said to himself.

"What are you looking for?" Crafter's voice said from behind.

"One of these blocks will give all the commands to the others," Gameknight said. "All of these are likely programmed to teleport the lava to the villagers, but somewhere among all these blocks is one that controls them all."

And in the darkness, binds them, he thought.

"Why don't we just start breaking the redstone?" Digger's voice boomed across the chamber.

Gameknight glanced over his shoulder and found his two friends running to catch up with him. Glancing up at the timer, the User-that-is-not-a-user saw that it showed 3.

"There's no time. I have to find the main control block," Gameknight said. *I have to hurry.* "You two can start breaking redstone. Every command block you disconnect represents a saved village."

Gameknight turned and tossed Digger his pickaxe, then dashed through the field of blocks. He tripped and fell over one. The light was dim and it was difficult to see. The only illumination came from the large pool of lava that was filling from a hole in the cavern wall, and the single redstone cube that blinked like his own heartbeat, fast and regular.

The level of the molten stone in the lava pool was almost to the height of the hole that spewed the fiery liquid. The sound of pistons moving echoed throughout the chamber. Glancing up, Gameknight could see the display now read 2.

I have to hurry, he thought. *Where would I put the main control block if I were going to teleport a bunch of lava from that pool to the villages?*

He concentrated as his gaze wandered across the pool of boiling rock, and then he saw it: a single command block set apart from the rest, sitting right beneath the pulsing redstone lantern.

"That's it!" Gameknight screamed as he dashed through the dim light.

Running as fast as he could, he streaked toward the beating lantern, ignoring the pain in his legs and chest. Glancing up, he saw the display change from 2 to 1. With all his might, he ran toward the lone block. He knew he wouldn't have time to break all the redstone that stretched across the floor. His only hope was to reprogram it.

Running with every ounce of speed, he shot past the last few command blocks. When he was two steps away, he dove through the air, his right hand extended. Landing with a thump, Gameknight drove his thoughts into the command block. He saw the code there and found the command he was looking for, /tp, and then he found the item code right after the teleport command. It was set to 10; lava.

He was so scared. If he didn't get this right, then everyone could be destroyed.

Thinking quickly, he put a new item ID number into the code, any number . . . 175 popped into his head. He replaced the code for lava with the ID number 175 just as the redstone lantern stopped pulsing and glowed with a constant intensity. The redstone traces leading from the lantern became alive with redstone power, making them all glow with an evil red light.

Standing, Gameknight watched as the redstone lines began to light up and spread across the large field of command blocks. It was like watching blood flow through the empty veins of some giant beast. The redstone traces grew brighter as the signal continued across the forest of command blocks. Glancing overhead, he could see the timer display now read zero. It was happening. He sighed.

"I hope I did it right," Gameknight muttered.

"We won't know until we go check," Crafter said.

"What about the skeletons?" Gameknight asked.

The young NPC pointed across the narrow bridge to the large cobblestone platform. Everywhere there were glowing balls of XP and white skeleton bones lying about. The white fur of the wolves shone bright in the dim light, looks of pride on their canine faces.

"The wolves took care of the skeletons," Digger said as he approached. "A few ran out of the cave, but a large pack went out hunting them. I don't think they will get very far."

Crafter moved to Gameknight's side and laid a reassuring hand on his shoulder.

"You did what you could," Crafter said. "Now we must go out and see what happened."

"First, we break all this redstone," Gameknight said as he pulled out a shovel and started breaking the glowing red lines.

As he worked, he could hear the other NPCs coming to join him. Soon the air was filled with the sound of tools breaking redstone, the glowing lines slowly being extinguished. When it was complete, Gameknight put away his shovel, crossed the narrow bridge, and stood on the large cobblestone platform. The NPC army surrounded him, all looking at him with uncertainty in their eyes.

"I wasn't able to stop the command blocks, but I did reprogram it, I think," Gameknight explained. "I just don't know if I did it in time or not."

"Then we'll go see," Butch said in a booming voice.

"No reason to hang around here and wait," Digger added, his voice competing with Butch's echoes. "Let's go."

Gameknight nodded, then turned and headed for the cavern entrance.

CHAPTER 28
GAMEKNIGHT'S REVENGE

Trapper led the group through the maze of tunnels back to the surface. They emerged from the subterranean passages where they had started, in the wide cutout that was carved into the side of Olympus Mons. Their horses were still tied to the fence posts someone had thought to place in the ground. Sadly, when they had first arrived at the mountaintop, they did not have enough mounts for all to ride double, but now it was no problem finding everyone a place on a horse.

Gameknight sighed as he realized how many had lost their lives in that underground battle.

Butch led the group away from the gigantic mountain and through the extreme hills biome. Moving at a steady trot, the group quickly rode out of the rocky landscape and into the flower forest biome.

They all breathed a sigh of relief when they entered the colorful woodlands. None of them realized how tiring it was to always be looking at the constant gray of stone and gravel that filled the last biome. But now, the bright red and blue and yellow flowers stood out in stark contrast against the lush green grass that covered the ground. It was a feast for their eyes.

The scores of wolves that followed the army quickly dispersed into the forest, happy to be out of the mountainous terrain and have soft grass under their paws.

"I am sad to see you go, my friends," Herder shouted to the animals as they disappeared amid the oaks.

"They did us a great service," Crafter said to the boy who rode behind him on a large, patchy black-and-white horse.

"I know," the Herder replied, a smile on his face.

"What about the other wolves?" Gameknight asked.

He looked down at the nine surviving animals that had accompanied them on this journey. Sadly, three had been destroyed in the battle. They looked up at the User-that-is-not-a-user with pride in their tiny eyes, their red collars standing out against their fur.

"These will stay with me until we get back home," Herder explained. "I've tamed them and they will not leave my side."

"Well, I don't mind saying it: I like having them with us," Hunter added. "It's always good to have a wolf around. You never know when you'll need one. Who knows what else is lurking out there, hiding in the shadows?"

"Perhaps you should send them out on patrol around our party," Crafter suggested.

"You're probably right," Herder said.

He scanned the pack for the largest of the wolves, then spoke a single word to the animal:

"Protect." Instantly, the alpha male barked once, then sprinted away from the riders, the other wolves choosing different directions and doing the same. In seconds, they had a furry protective ring around them. It made all the warriors breathe a sigh of relief.

Continuing on in silence, they party rode through the flower forest with bows in hand, eyes constantly searching the shadows for monsters. By sundown, they reached the lava-destroyed desert village that had been the first victim of Herobrine's revenge.

"Do you see anything different?" Crafter asked Gameknight999.

He surveyed the mound of cobblestone and obsidian.

"No, it looks the same to me," the User-that-is-not-a-user answered.

"That must be a good sign," Stitcher said.

"I doubt it," Gameknight replied. "Likely, this village was not targeted by one of the many command blocks in that chamber. It had already been destroyed and didn't need to be hit again."

"Maybe you're right," Stitcher said, then stretched her arms and yawned. Fatigue was taking a toll on all of their party.

"We'll camp here for the night," Butch said.

"Set up fortifications around the camp in case any more monsters decide to come pay us a visit," Digger added.

Gameknight looked at Crafter and smiled. Digger and Butch were used to being in command, and they both fell to the task with ease. This had brought the two of them together as fast friends. Now they commanded the army as one, neither vying for control, each just contributing wherever their strength could help the group.

The NPCs quickly placed blocks of stone around their encampment, taking what they needed from the sarcophagus that stood behind them, parts of it still warm.

After the sky had turned from its rich blue to a warm glow of reds and oranges, then to a star-speckled black, the camp became still as many went to sleep. But not Gameknight999. He was worried sick over the fate of the villages.

Did I change the code in time? Gameknight thought. *And what did I change it to?*

He'd been in such a rush that he really didn't remember the item number. But if he'd changed the ID number, from lava to something like sand or iron blocks, that could be just as deadly. At least Gameknight knew he hadn't set it to water, which would have been a catastrophe. Water had a single digit ID number and the User-that-is-not-a-user knew that he'd put in three digits . . . at least he hoped he had.

With sleep eluding him, Gameknight volunteered for the evening watch. He knew the wolves were out there, also watching, but the User-that-is-not-a-user felt it was necessary that one of them be awake and watching.

Moving silently through the camp, Gameknight listened to the sound of the forest. The bleating of a sheep and the occasional moo of a cow floated into the camp on the constant east-to-west wind. He heard no monster sounds, though, and none approached the resting NPCs, though he almost wished they had. Being alone with his thoughts was torture. Gameknight imagined every conceivable terrible outcome that could happen, all because of him, and it brought one horrific image after another as his mind played through all the possibilities. He was grateful when he saw the sky start to glow a soft orange as the sun's yellow face peeked up over the eastern horizon.

Gameknight woke everyone quickly, then began breaking down the barricades and fortifications they'd built at dusk. With practiced efficiency, the NPCs were heading toward Butch's village before the whole of the sun had made it into the sky.

They rode hard toward their destination, partly because it was far away, but also because Butch was nervous . . . no, scared. Everyone knew there were only two possible outcomes: his village would be destroyed like the last one, or it would be unharmed. There was no other option.

Shifting from a trot to a run, Butch goaded the group to move faster as they left the desert and moved into the rolling hills of his grassland biome. Ahead was a tall hill maybe a dozen blocks high. Gameknight remembered that the village sat just beyond that grassy knoll.

As they approached, Butch suddenly stopped.

"What's wrong?" Digger asked.

"I'm afraid," Butch said in a low voice, not wanting others to hear.

"I am, too," Gameknight added as he moved to the big NPC's side.

They looked at each other. Each could see the fear in the other's eyes.

"All of you stay here," Digger said. "I will go to the top of the hill and look. Just stay here."

Gameknight and Butch nodded, then watched as Digger rode up the hill.

His tall white horse ascended the grassy mound in two-block leaps, scaling the slope with ease. When he reached the top, he just stood there, staring down at the distant village, motionless, as if he were in shock.

"I'm not sure if that is a good sign or a bad sign," Butch said.

"I can't imagine how it could be a good one," Gameknight said. "But if . . ."

The User-that-is-not-a-user stopped speaking when Digger turned and motioned for the pair to join him on the peak. Gameknight and Butch looked at each other, fear in their eyes.

"I guess we have to do this," Butch said.

Gameknight said nothing, just nodded.

Urging their horses forward, the duo rode slowly up the hill, the rest of the army following close behind. Stitcher was suddenly at Gameknight's side. He was glad she was there. And then Hunter moved up on his other side, her red curls bouncing around her shoulders as she rode.

"We won't let you do this alone," Hunter said as she looked at him, compassion filling her deep brown eyes. He never noticed before how much the color of her eyes reminded him of rich chocolate.

"That's right," Stitcher added. "We're family and we'll do this together."

Gameknight said nothing as tears welled up in his eyes. He was so grateful they were here for him, in what could be the worst moment in his life. He was afraid.

As they reached the top of the hill, Gameknight closed his eyes, terrified.

As one, everyone gasped when they reached the summit, then remained silent.

"What is it?" the User-that-is-not-a-user asked.

"Open your eyes," Stitcher said.

"What happened?" he asked again.

Someone leaned next to him, then Hunter's soft voice whispered into his ear.

"Just look, you idiot," she said.

Slowly, Gameknight opened his eyes, then gasped.

Before him sat Butch's village, but instead of being covered with lava, it was covered with a field of sunflowers, the tall flowers growing from nearly every block of soil. Their yellow faces stared up at Gameknight, and he could have sworn they were smiling at him. And instead of this being the worst moment in his life . . . it was the best.

MINECRAFT SEEDS

All of the different biomes and structures mentioned in the book can be seen on Gameknight999's server. Just go to the book warp room at the old spawn and you'll see the buttons for each chapter. You can use the command */warp bookwarps*. I'll be building Herobrine's chamber somewhere on the server so that all of you can see what I was imagining while I was writing. Maybe I'll build Butch's village as well . . . come to the server and find out.

For those without access to the server, I've listed Minecraft seeds for version 1.87. I don't know if they will work with Minecraft PE or if they'll work for every 1.9; you'll just have to try them out and see.

Chapter 1: Crafter's village
Seed: 6154835779399006209

Chapter 3: Desert village
Seed: 1660196624

Chapter 4: Herobrine's Chamber

NOTE FROM THE AUTHOR

I really appreciate all the support I've been receiving from the readers sending me emails through my website, www.markcheverton.com, as well as people tweeting me @MinecraftAuthor, and on my Facebook page for Invasion of the Overworld. I love getting emails telling me how much people enjoy my books, and that kids are actually turning off the computer and reading . . . ironic, right?

We've seen lots of new activity on Gameknight's public server, as kids from all over the world are joining in to create fantastic shops and cities and fortresses. Quadbamber (LBEGaming on You-Tube), the developer of the server, has recently expanded the Gameknight999 server so that there is an epic lobby, fantastic new minigames, the popular survival server, and a new hardcore survival server (watch out for the flying creepers). But I think my favorite is still the creative server. I love watching kids create things out of blocks. Incredible pixel art sprouted up out of the ground one night and full 3D statues of the characters from my books have been built; I like all the versions of Crafter that I've seen on the different plots. You can find the IP address to the server on my website, www.markcheverton.com. Log in and look for me and my son, Monkeypants_271 and Gameknight999, and say hello. If you build something on the server and take a snapshot, I'll be posting all server-related images on www.gameknight999.com as well as posting important server information.

And as always, for those writers out there, keep sending me your stories. I've had some really fantastic ones submitted recently. I can see that many of you are writing more and improving your craft; the more you write, the better you get, and my editor, Cory, can attest to that with my own writing. Write, write, write . . . and don't stop. Please keep sending me your stories; I love reading them, and I post all of them on my website, www.markcheverton.com.

Keep reading, keep writing, keep creating . . . and of course, watch out for creepers.

Mark

AVAILABLE NOW FROM MARK CHEVERTON
AND SKY PONY PRESS

THE GAMEKNIGHT999 SERIES
The world of Minecraft comes to life in this thrilling adventure!

Gameknight999 loved Minecraft, and above all else, he loved to grief—to intentionally ruin the gaming experience for other users.

But when one of his father's inventions teleports him into the game, Gameknight is forced to live out a real-life adventure inside a digital world. What will happen if he's killed? Will he respawn? Die in real life? Stuck in the game, Gameknight discovers Minecraft's best-kept secret, something not even the game's programmers realize: the creatures within the game are alive! He will have to stay one step ahead of the sharp claws of zombies and pointed fangs of spiders, but he'll also have to learn to make friends and work as a team if he has any chance of surviving the Minecraft war his arrival has started.

With deadly endermen, ghasts, and dragons, this action-packed trilogy introduces the heroic Gameknight999 and has proven to be a runaway publishing smash, showing that the Gameknight999 series is the perfect companion for Minecraft fans of all ages.

Invasion of the Overworld (Book One):
$9.99 paperback • 978-1-63220-711-1

Battle for the Nether (Book Two):
$9.99 paperback • 978-1-63220-712-8

Confronting the Dragon (Book Three):
$9.99 paperback • 978-1-63450-046-3

AVAILABLE NOW FROM NANCY OSA AND SKY PONY PRESS

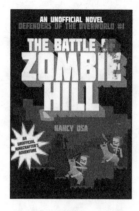

The Battle of Zombie Hill

Battalion Banished

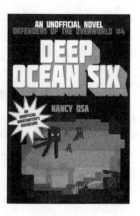

Spawn Point Zero

Deep Ocean Six

Available wherever books are sold!

AVAILABLE NOW FROM WINTER MORGAN AND SKY PONY PRESS

The Quest for the
Diamond Sword

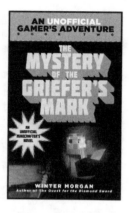

The Mystery of
the Griefer's Mark

The Endermen
Invasion

**AVAILABLE NOW FROM WINTER MORGAN AND
SKY PONY PRESS**

Treasure Hunters
in Trouble

The Skeletons
Strike Back

Clash of the
Creepers

AVAILABLE NOW FROM WINTER MORGAN AND SKY PONY PRESS

The Secret
Treasure

Hidden in the
Overworld

The Griefer's
Revenge

**AVAILABLE NOW FROM WINTER MORGAN AND
SKY PONY PRESS**

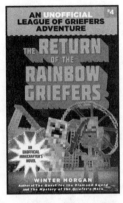

The Return of the
Rainbow Griefers

The Nether Attack

The Hardcore
War

Available wherever books are sold!

EXCERPT FROM OVERWORLD IN FLAMES

A BRAND NEW GAMEKNIGHT999 ADVENTURE

Ash clung to everything as the four companions rode through the charred wasteland. The wolves seem to get the worst of it, their fur collecting the ashen remains of the forest like iron to magnets, but they didn't seem to mind. Many of the cats, however, after being coated with soot, wanted to stop and clean themselves, but Herder kept them moving, encouraging them to follow with a high-pitched whistle.

As they moved through the burned-out forest, Gameknight saw many piles of blaze rods on the ground around them. That was strange. The golden remains of the blazes were far from where the fighting had been. Someone else must have been fighting in the forest...but who?

"Gameknight, look over here," Stitcher called out.

Steering his horse toward his friend, the User-that-is-not-a-user moved to her side. She had dismounted and was looking at a pile of something on the ground, the soot making the items difficult to identify. Stitcher took in a huge breath, then blew the ash away, the dark cloud billowing into the air. On the ground was a pile of snowballs, the icy spheres glistening in the morning light.

"Snowballs?" Gameknight999 asked, confused.

Stitcher looked up at him, then turned and looked at her older sister.

"Whatever this is, we don't have time for it," Hunter said. "Let's keep moving."

The younger sister swung back up into the saddle and kicked her horse into a gallop. After an hour, they made it through the dead forest and entered a cold taiga forest. Blazes had not attacked this biome yet, but being so close to Crafter's village, it was sure to be high on their list.

They shifted from a gallop to a sprint to make up some time. Soon, they came to a frozen icy river. Gameknight used his pickaxe to break through the top layer of ice so that they could get to the liquid below. Each of them took their turn jumping into the frigid waters. While they were washing the horses, Herder placed a block of wood on the ground and lit it with flint and steel. They then moved the animals near the fire to get warm after the chilly bath. The wolves eagerly jumped into the water to free the ash and soot from their fur, but the cats refused. Instead, they rolled around in the snow, cleaning as best as they could, then proceeded to bathe themselves with their pink tongues.

"Five minutes, then we get moving," Gameknight999 announced.

The others nodded as they rubbed their blocky hands together near the fire to get warm. They were all frozen, and the fire was a welcome relief. After the allotted five minutes, they mounted their horses. Herder leaned down and extinguished the fire, then followed Hunter as they continued to the west.

They rode through the frozen taiga in silence. Wolves howled at them through the trees, but Gameknight told Herder to keep his animals quiet. Stealth was likely their best weapon right now.

Following the spruce forest in the taiga was a desert hills biome. Gameknight always found it strange that a snowy environment could exist right next to the desert. Sheets of snow sat right up against scorching sand, and yet the temperature from the desert never seemed to bleed through into the taiga. It was just one of the strange and wonderful things about Minecraft.

As they moved through the desert, they all kept a keen eye out for monsters. Herder sent his wolves out away from the party, creating a protective ring of fangs and fur, while the cats always stayed close to their master. At one point, everyone turned to look as a bark came from one of the wolves to the right. A desert village was just barely visible through the haze, with a tall watchtower that stood high above the sandy village. They couldn't tell from this distance if there were villagers in the tower; it was just a hazy spire in the distance. But Gameknight knew there was no time to stop and check on them, for time was their enemy right now.

The trek continued in an uneasy silence for a couple of hours, all of the warriors scanning the terrain for threats. It was odd that they saw no creatures at all.

"I don't like this," Hunter said. "There should be a spider or creeper running around out here...but there's nothing. It doesn't seem natural."

"There are creatures out here," Herder said.

"Yeah, I know, your wolves and cats," Hunter replied. "That's not what I mean."

"I know what you mean, and you're wrong," Herder added.

"What are you talking about?" Gameknight asked.

"Creepers," Herder said.

"Where?!" Hunter snapped as she drew an arrow and notched it to her bow.

"Behind us. There's a group of them," Herder answered. "They've been following us for a while now. One of them is all sparkly and shiny."

"A charged creeper," Gameknight hissed.

They all turned in their saddles and looked back.

"You can just barely see them," Herder said, "but they're back there. They stay far enough away so they can just barely see us, which means we can barely see them."

"I don't see anything," Hunter said.

"Me neither," Stitcher added.

Gameknight strained his eyes, holding a hand over his brow to shield them from the sun. And then he saw it . . . a blue sparkle that looked like a flat sheet of lightning. The image shimmered for just an instant, then disappeared.

"I saw something. It must have been the charged creeper."

"What do we do?" Hunter asked. "I don't like having a bunch of monsters following us. Let's go get 'em."

"No, not out here in the open," Gameknight said. "They'll have too much time to start their ignition process. We need to trap them somehow. Let's just wait and be patient."

Hunter grunted her disapproval but turned back forward and continued to ride, glancing over her shoulder every other minute . . . watching. The presence of the monsters on their tail added an extra bit of tension to the group. They picked up the pace and shifted between a sprint and a gallop, hoping to add a little more distance between them and their pursuer.

They rode up and down the sand dunes as if they were sailing across ocean swells. Green, prickly cactus dotted the landscape like emerald sea serpents sticking their heads up out of the sandy waves. They added a splash of color to the pale surroundings, giving the harsh desert a sense of life and hope; something that was lacking in that burned-out forest around Crafter's village.

The User-that-is-not-a-user drove the horses hard through the desert. He wanted to get to the hive and get this business completed as quickly as possible, and the open countryside made traveling easy and fast.

After another hour, the party finally left the desert and entered an extreme hills biome. Steep stone cliffs and impossible outcroppings covered the landscape, most of which were impossible to scale. But *up* was not their destination; the creepers would be underground, hidden in dark tunnels and passages. In Minecraft, for some reason, the extreme hills biomes always had extensive tunnel systems running through the roots of the mountains. Those tunnels would lead them to the creeper hive and the secret pile of gunpowder that was hidden somewhere under the surface of the Overworld.

Weaving their way between rocky peaks, the party moved slowly through the terrain, the hilly landscape slowing their progress. They could see the blue of the ocean start to creep into view, the gentle waters stretching out until they met the blue sky. But as they rode through the rocky biome, the smell of ash grew stronger, biting the backs of their throats as they breathed. With no fires nearby, Gameknight knew there must be a large source of lava somewhere close. Moving past a large hill of stone and dirt, Gameknight was shocked at what he saw. A massive mountain came into view, with one side lit bright orange. In the dimming light of dusk, they had no trouble seeing the terrain, for a massive flow of lava was coming down one side and spilling into the ocean.

"We have to go *into* that?" Hunter asked.

"If you have a better idea, I'm listening," Gameknight said.

"How are we going to find the correct passage that will lead into the creeper hive?" Stitcher asked.

"I don't know.We'll just have to search carefully," the User-that-is-not-a-user said.

"This is a *great* plan," Hunter said sarcastically with a scowl.

"LOOK OUT!" Herder yelled suddenly.

Gameknight pulled back on the reins of his horse, just in time to stop himself from falling into a deep hole. Steering around it, Gameknight moved to a safe distance, then stopped to wipe his brow.

"Thanks, Herder," he said to his friend. "I think you probably saved me and my horse from getting badly hurt."

The lanky NPC beamed with pride.

"You know, that would be a perfect place for an ambush," Hunter said.

Gameknight looked at the hole and nodded his head. If they could just get the creepers into the hole, he thought, they could pick them off with their bows.

"How do we get them into the hole?" Stitcher asked.

"Bait?" Hunter suggested, looking at Gameknight with one side of her unibrow raised.

"You want me to go into the hole and wait for the creepers?" the User-that-is-not-a-user asked.

"Well—" Hunter started to reply, but was interrupted.

"My cats could get them into the hole," Herder said.

"What?" Hunter asked.

"Yep . . . they could do it," Herder said confidently. "Gameknight, you stand there on the other side of the hole. The creepers will come toward you, but my cats will force them into the hole."

"You sure?" Gameknight asked. "I'll be standing out there in the open like a sitting duck."

"A sitting *what?*" Stitcher asked.

"A duck," Gameknight replied. "You know . . . quack, quack, quack."

Hunter looked at him, then back to her sister and laughed. "I think he's losing it, for sure," she said.

Gameknight shrugged, then dismounted. He moved to the spot Herder pointed at, then pulled out a torch and placed it in the ground. With the darkening sky, the light from the torch cast a wide circle of illumination, making him easy to see.

"I hope all of you are going to be ready if this plan *doesn't* work," Gameknight said. "I don't look forward to fighting off two or three creepers at the same time. That's not my idea of fun."

"Whatever. Just quit your whining and stand there," Hunter said. She had moved behind a large mound of dirt and was hiding, ready to spring out in case she was needed. "Now be quiet. I can see them coming."

Gameknight999 moved next to the torch and stood there, waiting. He was sweating like crazy inside his armor, but yet felt freezing cold at the same time. He'd fought two creepers at the same time before, but he knew you have to time it just right: you had to hit one while you moved away from the other, to keep them from igniting at the wrong time. And if there were more than two . . . then he might be in trouble.

In the distance, he could see a flickering blue light begin to fill the dark shadows stretching across the ground from the setting sun. He couldn't see it yet, but the light was growing bright and brighter. And then the creature stepped out from behind a hill of stone and grass. It was a charged creeper, just as he thought, colored the normal mottled green but with a layer of blue electricity dancing around its body. This monster had been struck by lightning sometime in its past, and that electrical energy stayed with it, magnifying its explosive power. Charged creepers were dangerous creatures.

The sparkling monster scurried straight toward Gameknight, but as it came forward, more of its kind emerged from behind the hill. He gasped as he counted at least nine of them, every one heading straight for him.

Drawing his sword, Gameknight stood there and waited, fear nibbling at the edges of his courage.

COMING SOON:
OVERWORLD IN FLAMES:
HEROBRINE'S REVENGE BOOK TWO